A terrif
trapped ***throat.***

Blythe stared at the spot right outside the door where she could swear she'd seen the ghost of a man moving past.

No one there now. It had to have been nothing at all. Just her imagination playing tricks.

Blythe turned. But as she reached the foyer, *he* moved out of a shadow behind the door and into the light.

Oh. My. God. This must be the stalker. In the house!

Ashley. By now Blythe could actually hear the little girl's screams coming from out behind the house and she needed to reach her. But how to get past the stalker?

Time stopped, even as the alarm kept ringing and sounds of Ashley's voice continued to vie for her attention. But the stranger's stare felt stronger than all of that and it held her immobile. She began counting her own heartbeats as she fought to breathe. Those eyes of his were amazingly calm and penetrating. Cold steel gray, they studied her with dispassion.

Dear Reader,

Welcome to the world of THE SAFEKEEPERS, featuring the Ryans and their family curse. There's a slim chance that the curse can be lifted! But it will take two more good deeds by patriarch Brody Ryan. Time is growing short....

Second son Ethan Ryan has little concern for the family curse. Not being able to have children just makes his life easier. But this charmer will have to face his own demons in order to keep his clients *Safe by His Side*. He has a lot to learn, and I had a great time putting him through the wringer!

In *Safe by His Side,* I also continue my exploration of what it means to be a woman. When I began the trilogy, I came up with three traits I thought were representative of the best of womankind: courage, motherhood and love. In this second book, Blythe Cooper must overcome her preconceived ideas of both who she is and what it takes to be a real mother. She thinks fulfilling her job as a child's guardian will take her automatically to motherhood. Ah, if only it were that easy.

I loved taking THE SAFEKEEPERS to the glitz and glamour of Hollywood with this book. Mixing Mexican witchcraft with limos and the make-believe of TV production made for an interesting combination. One I hope you enjoy!

Happy reading!

With all my best,

Linda Conrad

LINDA CONRAD

Safe by His Side

Silhouette®

Romantic
SUSPENSE

SILHOUETTE BOOKS

ISBN-13: 978-0-373-27623-3
ISBN-10:   0-373-27623-0

Recycling programs
for this product may
not exist in your area.

SAFE BY HIS SIDE

Copyright © 2009 by Linda Sankpill

Visit Silhouette Books at www.eHarlequin.com

Printed in U.S.A.

LINDA CONRAD

was inspired by her mother, who gave her a deep love of storytelling. "Mom told me I was the best liar she ever knew. And that's saying something for a woman with an Irish storyteller's background!" Winner of many writing awards, including the *Romantic Times BOOKreviews* Reviewers Choice and the Maggie, Linda often appears on bestseller lists. Her favorite pastime is finding true passion in life. Linda, her husband and KiKi, the puppy, work, play, live and love in the sunshine of the Florida Keys. Visit Linda's Web site at www.LindaConrad.com.

To Tashya, with gratitude. You made me better.
Best wishes on new directions.

Prologue

"You son of a dog!" The witch's black words rang out in *Spanish under a rain-forest canopy on the Veracruz mountainside. "You have murdered my grandchild and banished my child. And your own children dare to join with you on this dark deed. I curse you all!"*

The old woman's words fell like poison darts on the ears of her victims. "Your punishment will match the crime, Brody Ryan." Black snake eyes watched from treetops and cold stars blinked in the heavens as her voice rang in the night air. "You shall never have the pleasure of seeing a grandchild. From this time forward, each child of yours will be barren. Your family will suffer for the sins of the father. Go to hell!"

The *curandera* Lupe Ixtepan Delgado slowly climbed down the mountain path from her mother's house with those hateful words of long ago still ringing loud and clear in her mind. She would do anything to help her grandchildren

escape the curses and hexes of her mother, the *bruja*. For
fifteen years Lupe had sought a way of making her mother
see reason. She longed to find a way to change the direction of her mother's blackened soul. The ancient woman
neared death, and Lupe didn't want her to die without
seeking God's forgiveness for the pain she'd wrought.

Yet the reversal of her mother's curse depended entirely
upon another. The man who had committed the original
crime must be the one to redeem himself before the curse
could be lifted. Lupe had no love for her son-in-law, Brody
Ryan. But she loved his children—her grandchildren—
beyond measure.

Brody Ryan was the key, and his children's salvation
might still be possible. He'd already managed one good
deed and had brought a needy child and its mother to their
destiny with Lupe's eldest grandson, Josh. Two more kind
and selfless acts from Brody Ryan, and Lupe's mother had
promised to reverse the curse on the entire Ryan family.

As Lupe wound her way home at the edge of her
maternal family's lake, she swore to keep a careful watch
over all the Ryan family. She wished that she could force
something good to happen. But when it came to Brody
Ryan's good or bad deeds, he held all the power.

Chapter 1

The evening sky over Beverly Hills grew ever more dull and gray as sea fog rolled across the 101. Soupy haze lent a chilly cast to what had been a warm spring day.

As the old song said, maybe "it never rained in Southern California." But Blythe Cooper would have much preferred a good thunder boomer to this creepy, opaque veil that uniformly covered palm trees, green grass and brilliant sunsets with its dark and somber mists.

Glancing at her winking computer screen, she tried to ignore the goose bumps running along her arms. She picked up the nearest file folder in preparation to continue her work. But her mind swung back to the murky shadows outside. She missed the old-fashioned, late spring thunder and lightning storms of her South Carolina childhood home. A good storm was exhilarating. It could take your breath away with its power and majesty.

Sighing deeply, she shrugged a shoulder and flipped open

her folder. Blythe had long ago decided she couldn't be happier to have taken this job as tutor-turned-guardian for child star Ashley Nicole Davis—even with the difference in weather. It was the job at which everyday, average Blythe Cooper had potential to be great. A job where her practical intelligence and her dogged eye for details meant she stood out and even excelled in the midst of all the fantasy, beauty and fanfare of the entertainment industry.

Here, she was needed and would be Ashley's rock in the storm. A solid presence was exactly what Blythe had been born to be, despite her rocky past.

A chilly air draft curled around her ankles and brought Blythe's head up from the stacks of travel plans and touring accommodations. Was there an open window somewhere? Both Ashley and the housekeeper knew better than to leave a window or a door ajar in inclement weather.

The house had felt especially gloomy ever since forty-year-old Melissa Davis, Ashley's mother, had been moved. Along with her twenty-four-hour nurses, Melissa now resided in the guesthouse on the other side of the pool, where she no doubt was sleeping off another round of chemotherapy treatments. Melissa would continue living out there for the remaining months—or weeks—of her life.

At some point after her mother passed away, little Ashley would be free to open windows and invite friends over and be as loud as she wanted to be in her own house again. Blythe wished for Ashley's sake that a miracle would happen and her mother could be cured. However, the most renowned physicians in the country had said there wasn't any possibility of Melissa surviving her illness.

Life did continue in this house, regardless of the impending death of its owner. Melissa had seen to that. The three other females still living in the house continued to work every day and dreamed of their futures, while Melissa continued to organize everyone and everything to her exacting standards from her deathbed.

According to her mother's wishes, Ashley would finish two more days of filming on the current season of her television show and then she would leave on the promotional tour for her summer movie. Mrs. Jenson, their housekeeper, would continue cleaning and cooking and taking care of the place as she had since the days of Ashley's first TV appearance. And Blythe herself would begin taking full responsibility for Ashley's personal well-being. Melissa wanted things to be that way.

Blythe had agreed to remain as Ashley's guardian after Melissa was gone. It was a long-term commitment, she knew, but Blythe had been both ready and happy to sign up. She'd grown to love Ashley over the last two years, and she would stand beside her in grief as she stood beside her in all of life.

Tired of the omnipresent depression that seemed to hang over the house, Blythe got up from her desk and went to search for the origin of the draft. She couldn't imagine where it might be coming from, but she supposed that seven-year-old Ashley's room might be a good place to check. She started down the long hall.

The house felt too quiet.

By this time of day, the housekeeper usually could be heard downstairs either making dinner or ordering out. As Ashley played in her room, her muffled giggles would dance gaily down the halls. And oftentimes the sounds Ash made as she memorized her lines along with the taped version the director sent over would provide a low-key and happy buzz to the atmosphere.

Not this particular late afternoon. This afternoon, you could almost hear the foggy mists creeping in through unseen cracks. As Blythe reached Ashley's half-open door, chills were already riding down the back of her neck. She eased through the doorway, half expecting to see her little star catnapping on the bed, though Ashley hadn't been interested in taking naps since before she'd turned five.

"Ash?" Nothing. The bed was littered with coloring books and stuffed toys, but no sign of a droopy seven-year-old fast asleep on top of the covers. And the French doors to Ashley's private balcony appeared to be closed up tight, too. So where was the draft coming from? And more important, where was Ashley?

Blythe stepped farther into the room for a closer inspection of the bathroom and the balcony. She needed to keep a closer eye on the little girl now that her mother had become incapable of most personal supervision. Especially now that the child star had begun receiving a few very odd pieces of fan mail.

Didn't it always work that way? Just when things looked darkest, something came along that had the potential for making it all so much worse. Ashley already had been dealing with her mother's illness and the somber reality of it when her guardians had been forced to cut off her Internet and free access to her fan mail because of a series of nasty e-mails and vague threats. Good thing Ashley was one tough kid.

As Blythe walked toward the bathroom, her attention was caught by a flashing dot at the top of Ashley's computer screen. When they'd cut off Ash's Internet, the technicians had set up an intrahouse circuit so that all the computers in the mansion could instant-message one another. But only one computer in the whole place— Blythe's—could still receive and send via the Internet.

To Blythe's surprise Ashley hadn't really minded the change. She'd learned to like having her own personal message system direct to the housekeeper and to her mother. And what made her the happiest was that she still had the ability to play all her video games.

So who was trying to reach Ashley via internal IM now? Was it the housekeeper, wanting Ashley to come down to dinner? Or could it be the girl's mother? And if so, was it something that Melissa Davis would need attending to right away?

Curious, Blythe sidestepped the bed and pressed the Enter button to read the message. There, against a cobalt-blue screen, came a six-line message in bold bloodred.

Twinkle twinkle little star
I don't need to wonder where you are
Come down to me from up on high
I promise you the world and sky
Don't fret, little girl, we'll be together soon
Come to me, Ashley, and I'll give you the moon

Blythe's stomach turned over and her palms grew clammy. This was the same kind of rhyme, done in the same chilling colors and with the same icky connotation, as Ashley had received before. The earlier ones were awful notes that usually ended with disturbing lines, sounding a lot like the overtures of a pedophile on the prowl. The police hadn't liked the tone of the letters and e-mail, but they'd said their hands were tied until the sender made an overt move.

To appear on Ashley's computer, this particular message had to have originated from somewhere within the house. That seemed pretty overt to Blythe. Someone was here. The evil had broken in despite their efforts to keep it out.

Oh, Ashley, where are you?

Ethan Ryan checked his watch as he kept one hand on the steering wheel of his rental car. He waited with his usual impatience for his sister to answer her cell phone back in Texas while he sat in L.A. rush-hour traffic.

"Where are you?" His sister Maggie was always in too much of a hurry for the niceties. No "Hello." No "How was your flight?" Just get right to the point. But that was okay by him. His own limited patience was legendary. It ran in the family.

"Sitting on the freeway in L.A.," he said grumpily to the baby sister who was, at least temporarily, his boss. "But I've got plenty of time yet. My appointment to meet with our new client isn't scheduled until seven thirty. I called you to double-check on—"

"Ethan, you have to get there *now.*"

"What's up, sis?" Ethan approved of his sister's and brother's efforts to save their deceased grandfather's business by turning his run-down private investigators' office into a security firm that specialized in guarding children. It was poetic justice, if nothing else. That's why Ethan had agreed to use his expertise to help them out. Well, that and the fact that he'd had to leave the Secret Service.

"You didn't move the appointment time up without checking with me, did you?" he blurted, not letting her answer the first question. "We were lucky the plane landed on schedule. This is the big city, Maggie. Not Texas. You just can't schedule things too tight. As it is, traffic will keep me on the freeway an extra—"

"I don't care how you do it, brother. But you have to be at Ashley Nicole Davis's house *right now.*"

"Have you heard something new from her manager? That, um…Grandpa Ryan's old college friend, what's his name?"

"His name is Max Slotsmeyer, as you would know if you'd read the complete info packet I put together for you. And no, he hasn't contacted me."

"Then why should I show up two hours early for a

scheduled appointment?" Ethan asked a little too irritably. "I wouldn't do that even if I could sprout wings and fly over this danged inconvenient line of cars. Which, as it happens, I can't."

"Ethan." Maggie lowered her voice to a whisper in order to capture his attention and make him listen. "Remember what *Abuela* Lupe used to say when she'd have a premonition—about feeling someone's bones walking across her grave?"

Ethan remembered all too well his maternal grandmother Delgado's special words and curses. Her witchcraft was part of the Mexican side of his family heritage. Most of the time he was glad about knowing *Abuela* Lupe's sayings and spells. But sometimes he wished he'd never learned them. His sister's tone told him this wasn't going to be one of the glad times.

"Yeah, I remember," he told Maggie. "And the connection is?"

"I'm feeling that same thing right now. Don't ask me how I know, but something is terribly wrong at Ashley Davis's house. They need you there. Please do something. You have to go now."

It would do no good to try talking practicalities to his sister. When it came to family witchcraft, spells and curses, they had all learned to accept each other's feelings and wishes unreservedly.

"I'll do what I can," he said in as soothing a voice as he could manage.

He hung up and took a breath before reaching for his briefcase on the passenger seat beside him. There hadn't been a reason to use any spells in a while. Not since the fiasco when none of his curses or magic would've worked to save him from an embarrassing and life-changing incident.

Abuela Lupe had spent most of their formative years

teaching him, his older brother and their younger sister the art of being *curanderos*—Mexican white witches—much to his very American-Texan father's chagrin. But when they'd entered their teen years, they'd begged *Abuela* to also teach them a few of the spells and curses of the black witches—the *brujos*.

By then the siblings had learned that hexes and blessings could be muttered with the same breath. And as teenagers, they'd wanted some of the fun of knowing black witchcraft. Ethan's young mind had reeled at the idea of getting any date he wanted with just the right hex, or raising his grade in any class with the proper combination of potions and herbs.

Their grandmother refused their request. According to her, black magic could not be trusted. They'd tried a few spells on their own and were fairly successful. In the long run, however, their immature white and black witchcraft hadn't turned out to be strong enough for *everything*. The brothers' and sister's magic had failed to make a difference when it had mattered most.

But today, Ethan felt sure he still knew enough magic to cause a break in this traffic jam. Enough of a break, that is, to transport him to his destination in a few minutes instead of hours.

Pulling a finger-size red amulet in the shape of an egg from a secret compartment in his briefcase, Ethan began channeling his powers. He reached into his memory for the right words to use and started an incantation.

Not sure what lay in store for him, Ethan nevertheless knew to trust his sister's hunches. If she felt it was imperative for him to be at Ashley Davis's house now, then his job was to make that happen.

Blythe quietly moved back to her office and picked up her cell phone to call the police. But as her hand hovered over the lighted keys, she remembered how unsympathetic they'd been the last time she'd called them about scary e-mails and letters.

They'd made her promise not to call again unless the threat was real and imminent. Could she swear an intruder was in the house now? She hadn't heard a thing, and the place did have a security alarm that was activated—most of the time. With a seven-year-old in residence, it was difficult to keep a security system set during the daylight hours. Still, there were no sounds at all.

Undecided about her next move, Blythe reached the top of the stairs with the cell phone still in her hand. She looked down the hallway in the direction of Melissa's old master bedroom, but decided she needed to check downstairs for Ashley first. This whole thing could just be a mix-up of some sort and in a few moments she would find Ashley sitting in the kitchen eating chocolate chip cookies.

Could Ashley have written the note herself as a joke? That didn't sound like something Ash would do, but you never knew. The girl did like making up her own poetry. She was a genius at some things, and she tended to be melodramatic at the best of times. Her mother's illness was the worst of times in Ashley's world.

Shaking her head sadly, Blythe pocketed the phone and headed down the stairway. Her best move would be locating Ashley and making sure she was not simply playing a game, since an intruder seemed impossible with the alarm system.

By the time Blythe reached the bottom stair, she had almost convinced herself that the spooky message was some kind of prank. Then she came to a sudden stop mid-thought, certain she had heard a noise this time. She froze in place, listening. Deadly silence was the only thing to reach her ears.

Blythe gave in to a momentary frisson of panic. Had she somehow failed in her responsibility to Ashley? No. Please, no. Refusing to believe that she'd messed up yet again, she set her shoulders and took another step. Before she angered Melissa by calling in the police, only to find Ashley had been acting out her grief by writing that note, Blythe decided her first move had better be to perform a thorough search of the house and grounds.

She headed toward the kitchen. Occasionally Mrs. Jenson gave Ash a treat before dinner. Those cookies, maybe, or a bowl of popcorn. Such things were not permitted according to Melissa's rules, but perhaps Blythe would find the girl trying to be extra quiet while she snuck in a forbidden snack.

Hitting the switch on the overhead spot lighting in the dining room, Blythe sought to dispel the claustrophobic feeling. She ran an uneasy hand through her hair, knowing it was useless to try to contain her noncompliant dishwater-blond curls. Between the humidity and the stress causing her to perspire, this was bound to be a bad hair day. No matter. Her life was filled with bad hair days. And how she looked was the least important thing on her mind at the moment.

Reaching out slowly to press against the swinging door leading to the kitchen, she caught just a hint of movement out of the corner of her eye. Blythe stopped and whirled in the direction of the French doors, which opened onto the terrace that ran around the back of the house. A terrified scream stayed trapped in her constricted throat as she stared at the spot right outside where she could swear she'd seen the shadow of a man moving past.

No one there now. Just her imagination playing tricks.

She let out a sigh. But then, just as her body began to relax, it seemed as though the whole world exploded around her in a whirl of noise. The doorbell rang, the alarm sounded and voices shouted.

Blythe turned and ran toward the front door. As she reached the foyer, *he* moved out of a shadow behind the door and into the light.

Oh. My. God. This must be the stalker. In the house!

Ashley. By now Blythe could actually hear the little girl's screams coming from behind the house. She needed to reach her. But how to find Ash without leading the stalker to her?

Time stopped, even as the alarm kept ringing. The stranger's stare felt strong and held her immobile. She began counting her own heartbeats as she fought to breathe. Those eyes of his were amazingly calm and penetrating. Cold, steely gray, they studied her with dispassion.

Blythe fought to speak, but no sound came out. She tried dredging up a little anger or indignation, *something* to hang on to and use in her defense. Still nothing.

The pressure in her chest expanded and she began worrying that she might pass out. But she had to do something. Hold him there to wait for the police and keep him from Ashley. A little girl's life depended on it.

Ethan tried to make sense of everything he was seeing and hearing. When he first arrived at Ashley Davis's house, he'd noticed that the front door was ajar. That looked wrong, and the foggy silence surrounding the place seemed somehow deafening.

He'd rung the bell on the way in, but he hadn't taken two steps inside the door when a big ol' devil wind broke loose. The alarm began sounding. Someone—was that a child's high-pitched voice?—shouted from the back of the house. And now this…this…schoolmarm-looking woman was standing there staring at him as if she were a mouse and he was the cat about to pounce. Well, hell.

"Where's the kid?" he yelled above all the din.

The woman's eyes grew wide, but she didn't make a sound.

"This is Ashley Nicole Davis's house, correct?" He took a step toward the woman. "Are you the housekeeper? What the hell is going on? Why's the alarm going off? And where is Ashley?"

Still nothing came from the woman's mouth. "Right. First we need to turn off that damned alarm." He headed off toward the back of the house and to the spot inside the back door where alarm installers normally placed their keypads.

He strode through the garishly decorated mansion and found the key-in pad exactly where he had expected. Seconds later, he'd used his magic to enter the right code to turn off the alarm. The kitchen phone rang and he picked it up, expecting the call to be from the security company. He was right. He identified himself, gave them the new password that had been prearranged and explained that he was already on the job and would complete a security check immediately. The company assured him that they had been notified of the change in procedures and about the new bodyguard and said they would stand by.

Ethan didn't waste another minute but started out in the direction of the earlier shouting. Whoever had been making all the noise must've been close to his current location, or maybe just outside the French doors to the pool and terrace. He followed his instincts at a trot, coming out of the kitchen into a wide family room at just the same moment as the woman he'd seen before came racing in from the other direction.

Well, at least she could actually move. Now if he could just be sure she could talk, too…

"Stop where you are," she shouted at him from about twenty feet back. "That alarm will bring the police."

He did a quick assessment. Noted she had no visible

weapon but did have a bulge in her dress's pocket that could be a tiny automatic—or more probably a cell phone. She was slightly above average height and slightly over average weight under that rather dowdy flower-print dress. Which meant her figure might be just a little on the lush side for his taste. Her brownish-blond hair ringed her head with a riot of soggy-looking curls, and her brown eyes were still on the wide and frightened side.

Nothing there that was too exciting, except maybe for the determined tilt to her chin. That was totally out of character for the rest of her image, and Ethan decided that one single attribute might be worth a second glance. Later. After he figured out what the hell was going on and found the child.

"Hang on, ma'am," he drawled, plastering on the wide grin that usually bought him whatever he wanted. "I've got it covered. I'm on the job now. But unless you can tell me that wasn't her yelling a moment ago, my first duty is to check on the welfare of Ashley Davis."

The woman turned and picked up a heavy lamp, ripping the cord from the wall. "Stay away from her." She hefted it above her head and moved toward him.

Well, that pretty well answered the question of the weapon in her pocket. But there was no time for explanations.

Making two quick maneuvers, Ethan forced her to drop the lamp. Then he pulled her back against his chest, tightening down on her in an incapacitating bear hug.

"Sorry I don't have time to play games, darlin'," he whispered. "Ashley comes first. So you and I are stepping out these doors right now to see if we can find her."

"Bastard," she hissed.

"Probably," he said, dragging her to the door.

The woman squirmed and kicked him hard in the shins. Ethan drew in a quick breath at the sharp pain, then

tightened his hold—maybe a little more than he should've.
He almost chuckled at the sound of her discomfort.

With a grunt of satisfaction, he pulled her even closer.
"Make that a *definitely*."

Chapter 2

Blythe squirmed away from the stalker the moment he dragged her outside the door. She could see Ashley and Mrs. Hansen through the lifting fog at the edge of the pool. With their backs turned to the house, the two were staring out past the pool house and across the wide lawn.

Blythe dashed toward Ash. Maybe the three of them could make a run for the pool house, lock the door behind themselves and call the police. The big lug who'd manhandled her didn't appear to have a gun. She and Ashley and Mrs. Hansen would just need to be faster than he was.

"Stop," the man shouted after her. "Don't any of you leave the patio. It might not be safe."

Blythe spun around at the sound of his voice, putting herself between the stalker and Ashley and facing him down. Too close, she thought. They would never make the pool house before he caught them. But he would have to go through her to get to her little charge.

"Go away. Leave us alone." Blythe pulled the cell phone out of her pocket and flipped it open. "I'm calling the police. You'd better run before they find you here."

"Good idea," he said with a wry grin. "I was just going to suggest calling, too. But first, maybe we should all introduce ourselves and find out what's been going on."

He took a step closer while pulling a flat, wide wallet from his suit pocket. At last Blythe gulped in a long breath and really looked at this man she'd assumed was a stalker. Wearing a dark business suit, a white button-down shirt and a red-striped tie, he looked more like an IBM employee or an FBI agent than a stalker.

"Okay," she said a little more breathlessly than she would've liked. "Who are you?"

"We saw a man," Ash interrupted as she came up from behind and took Blythe's hand. "Through the mist, coming down the balcony stairs from Mama's old room just as the alarm went off." She turned to the housekeeper. "Didn't we, Mrs. Hansen? We both yelled at him, but he ran away." Ash turned again and pointed out over the lawn. "That way."

The stranger went to Ashley's side and Blythe tightened her grip on the child's hand. "Ashley Nicole Davis? I'm Ethan Ryan, your new bodyguard." He knelt to be closer to her level and showed his ID. "Did you get a good look at the man? Can you describe him?"

"Nuh-uh," Ash said, and shook her head. "Too foggy."

Adrenaline draining from her body, Blythe went limp. She let the cell phone slip back into her pocket.

"Her bodyguard?" Trying to adjust to the new reality, Blythe dug deep for a little indignation to replace the fear. "You have a lot of nerve just waltzing into the house and scaring people half to death. There are rules of deportment, you know. Prospective employees ring the front doorbell and wait to be introduced. What are you even doing here at this hour?"

She'd known Max had hired a new bodyguard firm, against her better judgment. But Melissa had wanted them, so they'd been hired. "I thought your firm wasn't sending a man until we left on tour in a few days."

Ashley tugged at her arm while the bodyguard returned to his feet. "Blythe, Max told Mom he'd be stopping by tonight after dinner for our first appointment with the new man. Didn't you hear him say that?"

Shaking her head, Blythe blinked back the tears threatening to undermine her position. With one look into Ashley's wide violet eyes, Blythe remembered how much the child meant to her. What would she have done if the stalker had really gotten to the little girl? Confused and relieved, she was at a loss for words.

"Why don't we all go inside and see if we can straighten this out?" Ethan Ryan asked as he gestured toward the patio door. "In the meantime, I'll call the security firm and have them notify the police. I doubt that the subject will still be in the area, but the cops should do a thorough search anyway."

Still embarrassed and unsure of what her next move should be, Blythe took a breath and marched Ash to the kitchen doorway while Mrs. Hansen brought up the rear. The intense bodyguard stopped only long enough to study the door lock and the security wiring, then followed their small parade into the kitchen.

Mrs. Hansen, bless her, began chatting with Ash about dinner as the two of them walked into the pantry, totally ignoring what could've been a life-and-death situation. Blythe had a question or two for Ashley, but perhaps it would be better if she let the child have a moment to regroup first.

So…the new bodyguard. She turned, but found that he

was still on the phone with the security firm. Waiting for
him, she slid down onto one of the chairs at the industrial-
size kitchen table. Her shaky legs wouldn't have held her
up another minute.

As he continued on the phone, she took the time to
study the bodyguard named Ethan Ryan. Judging by
where she'd come to on his on his chest level when he'd
bullied her, Ethan had to stand at well over six feet tall.
At five-eight, she'd still had to tilt her chin to look up at
him. His rich, dark chocolate hair was styled short in an
almost military cut save for the suggestion of a curl at
his forehead.

He must've felt her staring at him, because he turned,
shooting her a steely glare while he finished up on the
phone. Ah yes, the eyes. A gunmetal gray, those tortured
eyes had been what had so captured her attention and made
her forget who she was and where she was going when
she'd first spotted him by the front door.

Really, he looked good enough to swallow whole, if one
was inclined to like the type. And he was exactly the sort
of guy Blythe had always fallen for in the past. But not this
time. Never again. She was through being used by good-
looking men who knew exactly what they did to women.

Just the thought made her mad all over again.

Ethan hung up the phone and tried a smile for the woman
whose stare had been burning a hole in his back, but her
scowl only deepened. "All right, then. The police will be
checking the neighborhood and they'll send a forensics
team over to search for fingerprints and to discover how he
gained entrance, but that'll take a couple of hours. In the
meantime, they don't want anyone to be by themselves."

When she only continued to stare, he took another tack
as he sat down across the table from her. "You must be the

personal assistant turned guardian. Uh…I'm sorry, but I didn't catch your name."

She lifted that strong chin again. "*Teacher* turned guardian. My name is Blythe Cooper and I was and still am Ashley's tutor before I became her guardian. And I—"

"Do you mind running over everything that happened right before I came in? I'd like to get a handle on what went down before the police arrive."

"Please don't interrupt. I would be happy to tell you what happened from my point of view, but I think you first owe me an apology for the rough treatment."

Ethan almost laughed at the prissy tone of voice. Man, this woman was something else.

"Did I hurt you?" he asked as politely as possible.

"No." She absently rubbed at her arms and Ethan actually experienced a moment's guilt. "But that's not the point. Why didn't you immediately identify yourself? And why did you feel it necessary to break in?"

"The door was open. Standing ajar. I rang the bell, called out and stepped inside to find out what was wrong." Ethan studied her movements carefully and decided her eyes were the key to what she was feeling. "Why didn't you answer me when I questioned you at the front door?"

"I didn't know who you were. I thought…I thought the stalker was inside. After I saw the note, I was—"

"What note?"

"Stop interrupting. Didn't anyone ever teach you any manners?" Gold sparks shot through those plain brown eyes as irritation colored her expression. Ethan found himself absorbed with the fascinating changes he observed in what he'd originally assumed was a rather ordinary face.

Just as he was about to give her another one of his charm-'em grins to get himself off the hook, Ashley and the housekeeper came back into the kitchen.

"Mrs. Hansen says she'll make my favorite dinner tonight. Isn't that cool, Blythe?"

Another more interesting change came over Blythe Cooper then. Her whole body seemed to soften as she stood to talk to the girl. The strict, set shoulders rounded as she hugged Ashley to her body. A smile lit up her face as if it were suddenly Christmas morning.

This wasn't simply a tutor turned guardian talking to her employer. Ethan hadn't seen anything like the transformation of Blythe's demeanor since…since before his own mother had died. It must be a kind of motherly thing he was witnessing. He didn't know yet how the little girl felt about Blythe, but the woman definitely harbored more than mere obligation inside her heart.

Interesting. And annoying. The simmering anger he'd buried from the day his mother died snuck up on him and left him trying to hide his emotions. Again.

"Are we talking chicken nuggets and French fries?" Blythe teased Ashley in a low, smoky voice that suddenly fueled Ethan's fantasies in a decidedly non-motherly way.

Well, sexual urges might be one method of relieving his old annoyances and pain. But with the rather dowdy guardian? Maybe he needed a day off instead.

"Yes!" Ashley said in a loud whisper. "And chocolate ice cream with rainbow sprinkles. But don't tell Mom."

Blythe moved back a step but still had a faint smile on her face. "Not a chance. Your mother doesn't need to think about such things tonight.

Blythe slid easily into a totally different tone. "Where were you and Mrs. Hansen coming from when you noticed that man? What were you doing outside the house?"

Ethan's senses picked up on the subtle change in Blythe's demeanor. A casual question for the girl's benefit belied the seriousness of the subject. Blythe's protective instincts seemed to scream silently from her every pore.

"Excuse me, but where is Ashley's mother?"

"My mom's sick," Ashley told him.

He bent down on one knee again. "I heard that, sweetheart. I'm sorry."

"They moved her into the pool house this morning. She said she didn't want to disturb me anymore. But I wasn't disturbed. I just had to be quiet while she slept. And I had to stay in my room or with Blythe, but only when they were giving her the treatments. It was lots better that way than having her in the hospital all the time." Ashley's wide eyes glazed over, but Ethan sensed a strength underneath them that surprised him.

He could think of several more things to ask. About the relationship between mother and daughter. About the relationship between child and guardian. But for the moment he decided to stick to the point.

"So you'd gone out to visit with her when all the noise started?"

Ashley nodded, and Mrs. Hansen the housekeeper spoke up from across the room. "It was my fault, sir. I was running late in bringing dinner out to the nurses and I asked Ash to help me carry the dishes so it wouldn't take so many trips. I'll do better when we get the schedule down."

Ethan straightened up and addressed Mrs. Hansen, making sure Ashley could hear as well. "I don't see how either of you made any mistakes, ma'am. Ashley ought to be able to visit her mother whenever she wishes without being afraid.

"Do either of you remember anything special about the man you saw?"

"It was like Ash said," Mrs. Hansen began hesitantly. "The fog was really thick. I only got glimpses of a dark shadow moving down the stairs. If the alarm hadn't started going off, I don't think I would've noticed him at all."

"Okay." Ethan gave her one of his crooked smiles—reserved especially for female clients. "But the police are probably going to ask both of you these same things. If you think of anything at all about the man's appearance, be sure to tell them."

"Are the police coming?" Ashley asked Blythe. She began blinking wildly. "Mama won't like that."

Blythe went to her again and gave her a hug. "We'll only tell your mother if we have to. Let's wait and see what the police have to say. And since Uncle Max is coming by in a little while, we'll check with him, too, before we say anything to upset her.

"You know that's the real reason the doctor wanted your mom moved, don't you?" Blythe added softly. "It wasn't anything to do with you. She needs to stay quiet and not be bothered by phones or visitors and such upsets. You know, like the stuff that goes on around here most of the time. And it was your mom who decided on the pool house instead of returning to the hospital just so you could visit any time you wished."

Ashley hung her head and swung her body from side to side. "I know. But maybe if I stopped acting for a while, it wouldn't be so noisy around here. All the reporters and photographers would go away and leave us alone."

She glanced up at Blythe and apparently saw an answer she'd heard before. "Oh, I know. Mama doesn't want me to quit. And I really do love acting. Really. It's just…"

Ethan's heart went out to the child as her words ran down. She looked nothing at all like the huge megastar Ashley Nicole Davis. With hair stringing down to hide her face and her chin resting against her chest, she looked like what she was—a lonely little seven-year-old whose mother was dying. He nearly asked why she couldn't quit if she wanted to, but figured he had better keep his mouth shut. That wasn't any of his business. His job was to keep her safe. Period.

He turned to Blythe. "I didn't see any reporters outside when I pulled up. Are they here most of the time?"

Instead of answering him, Blythe kissed Ashley on the forehead. "Don't worry about anything, honey. It will all work out the way it's supposed to. Why don't you stay and help Mrs. Hansen make the supper while I take the new bodyguard upstairs to talk for a minute? Okay?"

"Can I?" The little girl's face brightened immediately. "I don't have to go back to my room?"

Blythe whispered quietly to the child for a second and then motioned for Ethan to follow her out of the kitchen.

When they were out of Ashley's earshot, she explained, "We're doing our best to keep those terrible tabloid reporters away for the present. As far as they know, there's nothing newsworthy going on here. We want to keep it that way. The reporters and photographers upset Ashley. And Melissa doesn't want them to get wind of how bad her illness is just yet, either."

"Okay." There was something else behind her words. Ethan had the feeling it was personal, but again, asking wasn't his job. "Where are we going?"

She started up the wide staircase. "I want to show you something before the police arrive. It's one of the things we need to keep hidden from the tabloids. And I'd rather Ash didn't have to see it."

Ethan dogged her steps up the stairs. He tried cataloguing in his mind everything he'd learned so far but got distracted by Blythe's generous backside as she climbed each stair above him. His first choice in women tended toward the ultrathin model type. The kind that looked sexy in their push-up bras and little-boy briefs. But he found himself admiring Blythe's rounded curves a lot more than was appropriate.

Maybe it'd been too long since he'd had any woman. What with his recent "female" problem, he'd not even considered taking someone out just for fun. And thinking *that* way about this woman, a client and an irritant, would make him too stupid to live.

Hadn't he learned a lesson from the fiasco that had cost him his career? Stay totally professional with the female clients, he chided himself. Professional. Period.

"So, I understand Ashley has received other notes like this one."

Blythe maintained the five-foot invisible barrier she'd erected between herself and Ethan. "Yes. She'd gotten several e-mails similar to this one before we cut off Ash's Internet access. And the same sort of disgusting stuff in handwritten notes, too."

When he just shook his head and checked the computer, she continued. "We've had to hire a fulfillment firm to open Ashley's fan mail and a new business firm to handle all the other mail that arrives. We no longer receive any mail here at the house. And my computer is the only one that can send or receive e-mail."

"The police have copies of the other correspondence?"

She nodded and then folded her arms over her waist to keep herself together. "The notes are the reason Max and Melissa decided to hire new bodyguards. But this one had to have come from somewhere inside the house. It nearly scared the life out of me when I found it."

"I can imagine." Ethan turned his attention to her, and the sensual glint in those gorgeous eyes hit her full blast. "I'm beginning to understand why you were so frightened at seeing a stranger inside the house.

"You have any guesses as to which of the house's computers might have been used to send this note?" His gaze went from sexy to concerned to all business and threw her into another kind of tailspin.

She worked to keep herself from stammering. "Probably Melissa's old computer, the one located in her suite." It had to be. All the others would have been in places too difficult to reach without being seen.

"In the rooms she vacated this morning?"

"Yes." Blythe felt like an idiot. Ethan was so spectacular looking and she was so *regular,* probably a hundred and eighty degrees from his usual type of women. She'd met a few actors in the course of her job who were as good looking as Ethan, but none of them had ever gazed at her with quite that kind of intensity.

Fighting the urge to fall at his feet, Blythe reminded herself of her two previous failed attempts at finding love with gorgeous, charming men. With a jolt of self-deprecation, she pushed her shoulders back and reverted to her normal, confident attitude.

"I haven't had time to contact the computer gurus to come unplug it yet. Come on. I'll show you."

When she led him into Melissa's old rooms and to her computer setup, Ethan reminded her not to touch anything. Then he asked to see the French doors that went out to the balcony and the stairs leading down to the pool.

He studied the door and the lock without using his hands. "Doesn't look like anyone broke in this way. But someone definitely set off the alarm when they opened this door from the inside without disabling the system. Maybe the police will be able to pull fingerprints from in here."

A chill rode down her spine. Someone really had been in the house with her. And this close to Ashley, too.

What if Blythe had turned to check out Melissa's suite

before she checked downstairs—would she have run into the real stalker? The thought clogged her throat for a moment, and then anger took over. Refusing to cower to a stalker's deliberate attempt to paralyze them with fear, she vowed to start carrying pepper spray or a stun gun in her pocket. She also made a promise that from now on someone would keep Ashley in sight at all times.

Ethan recaptured her attention. "But the alarm wasn't sounding downstairs and someone had opened the front door. Do you think it might've been Ashley and the housekeeper?"

Her gaze slipped to his mouth and her own mouth started watering at the thought of how kissable his lips looked. "Um…no. I'm sure the two of them left by the patio door." This ridiculous stammering and daydreaming over a near stranger's sexy appearance simply had to stop.

He nodded thoughtfully. "Zone alarm system. The upstairs wings must be on separate systems but integrated into the main alarm. However, that still doesn't answer how someone got through the locked front door.

"You'll need to make a list of anyone who has keys to the house. I'll have the alarm firm come out tomorrow, change the pass codes and rekey all the doors."

Ethan reeked of professionalism. But as much as she'd decided Ashley needed a bodyguard, Blythe didn't want it to be this ultracharming one. She couldn't wait for Max to arrive so she could demand that he ask the bodyguard firm to send a different man. Ethan Ryan and his sexy eyes simply had to go.

Chapter 3

"He's a part owner of his family's investigations and protection business," Max explained after Blythe told him that she wanted Ethan replaced. "And the best bodyguard available. Until a few weeks ago he worked for the U.S. Secret Service—the presidential detail. They're the most elite bodyguards in the nation. We couldn't ask for a better man to guard Ashley."

"But…" Stuck, Blythe couldn't manufacture a good enough reason to get rid of the guy in view of this information. She'd wanted to say she could take care of guarding Ashley herself. After all, Blythe felt competent at almost everything where Ash was concerned. But not this time. She certainly could not compete with a member of the elite presidential bodyguard detail.

Max patted her arm as they sat together on Melissa's huge theater-room sofa. "I've known his family for a long time. Since before he was born. His grandfather was an old

friend. I'd like to lend my support to the security firm
Ethan and his brother and sister are trying to get off the
ground. They're good people. They deserve a shot.

"Look," Max continued in his gruff but congenial voice.
"Ethan may have had a bit of trouble in his life, but as far
as I can tell, none of it has been his fault. Maybe you two
just got off to a shaky start and can overcome it. What do
you say we give him another chance? Ashley needs the best
bodyguard available."

Max Slotsmeyer had to be in his mid-seventies, but he
was still every bit as sharp as a row of shark's teeth. At one
time everyone in the business had even called him the
Shark. He'd been one of the best entertainment attorneys
in the world, but today he had cut his client list down to
one. He still managed Ashley's career, but only because he
and his wife were like grandparents to Melissa. They'd
taken her and Ashley in when Ash was a baby, after
Melissa's husband had been killed in a car accident.
Without Max, Blythe didn't imagine Ashley would've ever
made it to megastar status.

Blythe liked and respected Max. In fact, she owed her
job to him. When she'd made that hideous mistake about
a year ago, Max had interceded on her behalf with Melissa.
With that in mind, and especially knowing Max was set on
it, Blythe decided to suck up whatever problems she had
with Ethan and give the guy a second chance.

"Okay, Max. I'll try to be more forgiving. It's not like
I've never made a mistake, is it?"

Max chuckled. "Good girl. I know you want the best for
Ash. We all do. Where's Ethan right now?" he added in a
change of thought.

She shrugged. "I think he's still out combing the neighborhood with the Beverly Hills police."

"That's fine," Max said as he stood. "I'm going over to

visit with Melissa for a few minutes. Maybe I'll catch him on my way back. If not, make him comfortable here. Give him whatever he needs to do his job."

Max stood and reached into his breast pocket for the ever-present cigar. Blythe had never seen him light up, but he carried one in his fingers at all times. Apparently old-time Hollywood agents and managers considered expensive Cubans to be part of the uniform of the day.

Blythe murmured her thanks and watched Max lumber toward the patio door on his way to the pool house. Now she had no choice but to find a way of dealing with Ethan.

Ethan worked into the night, setting up the intercom system between Ashley's bedroom and the guest room located two doors away. With the over-the-phone assistance of the security-alarm firm, he'd reset the alarms on all four zones. Tomorrow at 6:00 a.m. the company was sending a team to rekey the doors and adding an additional security man to guard the front gate.

Ethan's job description called for him to stick with Ashley. But he was smart enough to know that even children needed a little space. He remembered from his presidential duty that having ever-present security hovering over your shoulder could be just as stressful as a stalker. So he had come up with the idea of moving the previously unused baby-intercom system from Melissa's master suite bedroom into the guest room where he would be spending nights.

When he plugged in the last of the wires, the first thing Ethan heard over the line was Blythe tucking Ashley into bed. He couldn't make out the girl's words, but Blythe spoke in soft, soothing tones. It surprised him when her husky, low whispers seemed to wrap around his body like a lover's thighs. His skin buzzed with physical awareness and he caught the brunt of shocked awakening straight in his groin. Hell. Where did that come from?

Leaning back in the guest room's overstuffed chair, he fought his response by closing his eyes and keeping one ear out for any trouble. A few reminders of the job he hadn't been all that happy to take in the first place ought to do the trick and bring his body back under control.

Blythe was reassuring Ashley. "We're safe and your mother is getting the best care," she told the child. "You have two more days left until shooting ends for the season. You know what your mother expects. Nothing's happened tonight that should change that."

"But, Blythe—"

"Nuh-uh, honey. It's not time to goof off yet. We'll get a few days free while we're on tour this summer, I promise."

"But I want to spend tomorrow with Mama before we have to leave town."

Blythe tried to convince the little girl that her mother would rather Ashley do her job and live up to her obligations. But the quiet words bothered Ethan. Obligations at seven years old?

At Ashley's continued objections, Blythe's tone began changing from soothing and sexy to stern. It made Ethan think back to times when his own mother had tried convincing him to keep on working at whatever summer job or afterschool chore his father had forced on him at the time. But it was his father's words from those long-ago days that still rang over and over in his ears all these years later.

"You're a worthless bum," Brody Ryan used to tell him. "You'll never amount to a dime."

Thinking back on it now, Ethan had seemed determined to prove his old man right. Before his mother died, he would cut school, get drunk and drive his pickup wildly through the countryside shooting up road signs with a rifle.

He'd even dabbled in black witchcraft and tried dope. Anything and everything his father might consider trouble.

But after his mother died in that plane crash, all Ethan could remember being was angry. Mad at his mother for leaving and furious at his father for caring more about the ranch and money than he did for his children.

The last thread to Ethan's wild childhood had been cut about six months after his mother's death when his father packed up their beloved grandmother, *Abuela* Lupe, and carted her off to his maternal family's ancestral home in Mexico. Lupe's mother, his great-grandmother—the black witch of Veracruz—had promptly cursed the entire family in her anger over the mistreatment of her daughter. And the curse had taken hold. Brody Ryan would have no grandchild. Ethan, his brother and sister would all be sterile from that day forward.

Ethan hadn't really paid much attention to the family curse. His whole life had felt as though it were cursed anyway. What did it matter to him if he couldn't have children? Great. One less worry to slow him down on his way to the freedom of adult life.

When Blythe's raised voice came irritably through the intercom, Ethan focused back on the present. "Enough now, Ash," she said. "You *are* going to work in the morning as usual, and we *will* be leaving on schedule for the tour. Period. Now go to sleep."

Ethan shifted in the chair and kicked off his boots, listening as Blythe could be heard checking the child's windows and shutting the hall door on her way out. The woman was simply too serious and demanding to be a child's guardian. Her tone had ended up sounding more like a drill sergeant's. The fact was, Ashley probably deserved a day off after tonight's excitement. Give the poor little kid a break. Her mother was dying, after all.

Annoyed with Blythe again, and with himself for having inappropriate physical reactions to someone he had to work with, he began wondering about Blythe's background and how she'd ended up here. Ethan settled in to wait until the rest of the house went quiet for the night. Until he could recheck the perimeters and triple-check all the alarms. There wouldn't be much sleep for him tonight, but he didn't require much.

As he waited, he decided to review the file on Blythe Cooper that Maggie had sent along with the files on Ashley and Melissa Davis. Ethan's new sister-in-law, Clare, was a real geek when it came to ferreting out background info. She'd been a reporter before she and her son had gone on the run from her ex, and maybe that explained her excellent instincts when it came to digging up important intel. Ethan rather liked his brother's wife and was glad to have Clare both in the family and at work in their new security business.

He opened the report on Blythe and thumbed through the pages he'd only skimmed on the plane ride out here. Blythe Cooper, age twenty-seven, had been raised in a college town in South Carolina by her mother and father, both college professors. Her older brother was one of those child-prodigy geniuses who'd graduated from college at age seventeen and had gone on to do physics research and now drew exterior designs for NASA. Blythe's younger sister also had a high IQ, but her main interest seemed to be winning beauty pageants. Currently, the sister was Miss South Carolina and headed for the Miss U.S.A. pageant.

Quite the family tree for a plain Jane like Ms. Cooper.

Blythe herself had graduated from college, but at a more sedate pace. She'd earned a master's degree afterward in education, had taught elementary school and managed to win a Teacher of the Year award before quitting and coming to California to become Ashley's tutor a couple of years ago.

On the personal front, Blythe had been a studious teenager and had no trouble in school. Well, that seemed right—and about as far from his own background as could be. After college she'd married a Ph.D. candidate whom she'd met through her parents. The two had divorced a few months before Blythe accepted the tutor position.

The pages of Blythe's report ran out there and Ethan closed the file. Not much to go on to explain her attitude thus far. And certainly nothing to explain why the sound of her voice and the tilt in her chin caused him to suddenly become so aware of her. It made him wonder what she'd done besides work since moving to California. Had his sister-in-law missed something important from Blythe's personal life over the last few years? Did this woman have a secret life that would explain why he felt so tense around her?

So far she'd been as annoying as hell to him. But even with that, there was something about her that reached out to him and made him curious. Because he couldn't imagine why he felt the way he did. Blythe didn't look a thing like his normal choice of female companion, and her background didn't appear to have been complicated or demanding. By the sound of that report, she was just what she appeared. Perhaps she'd been born into an extraordinary family, but the divorced teacher turned tutor turned guardian wasn't anything to write home about.

Still…there was something.

Yawning and becoming resigned to working with her regardless of how he felt, Ethan hoped the police would be able to get a line on the little girl's stalker soon so he could turn the job over to someone else and go on to the next thing.

Still not sure the direction the rest of his life would take after this assignment, Ethan was positive of one thing. Working with Blythe Cooper had to be just a short-term arrangement.

Despite the fact she hadn't gotten a whole lot of sleep, Blythe woke up at 5:30 a.m. clear-eyed and ready to face the day. Yeah, and what a great day, with Ashley acting irritable and anxious and with herself having to face the new bodyguard again.

Terrific.

Suddenly grouchy, Blythe headed for the shower. She had lain awake most of the night hating herself for the tone she'd had to take with Ash at bedtime. The child was usually so good and sweet and never caused anyone a moment's problem. But of course that was all back before her mother had moved out to the pool house to die and then refused to let Ashley slack off from work for even so much as one lousy morning.

It wasn't fair. But then life wasn't fair, was it? If life always turned out the way you wanted, then Melissa wouldn't be dying and there would be no stalker to threaten a little girl star—and no need for a bodyguard to drive Blythe right up the wall.

But Blythe reminded herself that the best plan, the only plan, was for her to deal with Ash as gently as possible, and to deal with Ethan from a distance until the threat was gone.

Twisting the water faucets to hot, Blythe stripped and stepped under the spray. Trying not to think of the man, she soaped up and thought of him anyway.

Since the first time she'd seen him standing there in the shadows, Blythe had acknowledged that he must be one of the world's top ten best-looking men. With his firm, solid jawline, the golden skin tone that spoke more of a Latin heritage than his Irish name might suggest and those wicked gray eyes—eyes that seemed to take in everything and could go from charming playboy to dedicated bodyguard in an instant—Ethan Ryan would be a hard man to forget.

As hot water sluiced over her body, carrying soap bubbles down through every crevice, flickers of sexual tension licked across her belly. She absolutely refused to allow any such feelings. Blythe had long ago given up reacting to a pretty face and a charming demeanor. After last year's fiasco, she'd sworn never to let another charmer worm his way under her defenses.

Never again. Her job, her relationship with Ash and her ego would never make it through another disaster as bad as falling for someone like that. Twice in her life was more than enough for any sane woman, thank you.

She twisted off the water and began towel-drying her hair. Going about the business of getting dressed for the day, Blythe tried to regroup so she could manage to face Ethan without letting him find any cracks in her facade.

Since Ash's series production company would be shooting exterior shots for the last time today, Blythe decided to pull on a pair of jeans and a cotton sweater. After wrestling with the wild tangles on her head for a few minutes, she finally gave up and pulled it all back off her face with a fuzzy rubber band. Not a particularly flattering look for her she knew, but practical and easy.

With a slow, deep breath, she drew herself up and felt ready for anything. Until she stepped out of her room and stumbled at the surprising sight of Ethan, awake and dressed and standing in the hallway as though waiting for her. Bracing a hand on the wall, she had to take another deep breath before she could speak.

Leaning back against the threshold to Ash's room, he stood with his arms folded, his chin set and those gray eyes watchful. Ethan didn't so much as move an eyelash when he spotted her. With hair still slick from shower dew, a freshly shaven face and his chambray shirt sleeves rolled halfway up his arms, the bodyguard looked every bit as dangerous as a German shepherd guard dog. More so, because of what the sight of him did to her libido.

"What are you doing?" she demanded in a stage whisper. "Is something wrong or are you just being extra careful? Ash can't be in that much danger inside her own room."

With movements slow and deliberate, Ethan took her elbow and stepped two yards down the hall before he turned to speak. "Everything was quiet in there until about ten minutes ago. From the sounds of things, Ashley is up and moving around and may have been using her computer. It's my job to be extra careful until the doors are rekeyed and a guard is in place on the gate. I'm here in case she needs anything."

"You think the stalker might've left another one of those messages for her?" The thought made Blythe's skin crawl. "It wouldn't be possible unless he got into the house again somehow."

Ethan's jaw clenched. "No, that's not what I think." The intensity of his stare made her feel itchy and vulnerable. But her job wasn't the only one on the line here, so she straightened her spine and lifted her chin as she got ready to let him have it.

Before she could open her mouth, he seemed to settle for a shrug. "Why don't you go on in and check Ashley's computer? See for yourself."

Everything inside Ashley's room seemed perfectly sound. The girl was in her bathroom, brushing her teeth and getting ready for the day. The note still blinking on the computer screen had come from her mother, reminding Ash of the day's shooting schedule, what she should wear to the studio and that she should pay attention and do whatever the new bodyguard told her to do.

Blythe gritted her teeth. The irritation she automatically felt because of Melissa stepping onto her turf must be set aside. Blythe knew this note was nothing more than a last desperate grasp for the parental control that Melissa realized was slipping through her fingers for good.

Blythe was still plenty annoyed over Ethan's earlier smug arrogance, and also that sensual glint in his eyes when he looked her way. But she didn't want any of that to cost her the job she loved.

Vowing to stop letting him get to her, Blythe helped Ash get ready. At the last moment she found the day's script pages stuffed under Ash's bed, put them in her briefcase and then managed to grab them both a glass of OJ on the way out. Despite Blythe's annoyance and her growing foul mood, she let Ethan usher them through the front door when the studio limo arrived to take them to the back lot.

This was going to be one hell of a long day.

As the limo pulled away from the Davis mansion's cul-de-sac and headed toward Sunset Boulevard, a man huddled behind the wheel of his five-year-old Ford down the block and watched. Hidden beneath thick bougainvillea and oleander in the driveway of a neighbor who was out of town, the man took no notice of the morning's sapphire-blue sky or the sweet, romantic scent of orange blossoms perfuming the Southern California air.

He'd seen enough to give him several new directions to follow. He had slowly worked at setting this plan in motion over the last month or so, and every detail needed to be perfect for him to get what he wanted.

Last night's "stalker" note and the commotion that had followed had actually seemed to be accomplishing just what he'd hoped. Then a few hours ago he had been disappointed when the police left after only a cursory search. That kind of reaction wasn't nearly good enough. They'd given up too soon. He would need to ramp up the tension.

But his plans were taking shape. The goal was in sight.

Chapter 4

"Wow!" one of the production assistants whispered loudly as the group of young women standing at the crew's catering table all turned to stare. "Someone get me a camera. Anyone have a cell phone handy? That dude is seriously yummy. Who is he?"

Immediately two cell phones appeared, one having been pulled from someone's short's pocket and one unbelievably slipped out of a bra, and both started snapping shots in a fury. Amazing how those phones had been so handy, since the director had banned cells from the set. Blythe cringed and ducked her head.

It had been a long morning, just as she'd predicted. Ash had fussed and squirmed all through makeup, and uncharacteristically hung back when called to the set. Now the little girl had gone to work with her vocal coach, whom she loved, and Blythe had taken the opportunity to have some badly needed coffee.

She finished pouring herself a cup and tried not to be embarrassed by Ethan Ryan being the center of attention. Although, in black jeans, a black tee and the gray suede jacket that he'd changed into before they'd left that morning, he *was* seriously yummy looking. He stood by himself about ten yards away from the table, with his feet spread at attention and hands behind his back, silently waiting for Ashley. If Blythe dared to deny knowing him, eventually the truth would be found out. So she decided to join the gossipers.

Clearing her throat, she hoped to switch their attention in another direction and off the man. "He's Ashley Davis's new bodyguard. His name is Ethan Ryan."

All four women turned to stare at her. She had never before been the focus of their attention. In fact, she wasn't sure they'd ever noticed her at all. The idea that the charming bodyguard could make such a splash with these sophisticated movie crew types made her nervous. But she had to be careful what she said.

Blythe needn't have worried. Ashley was the last thing on their minds.

"Where'd he come from?" the grip assistant with the long auburn hair asked.

"What's his background?" the twentysomething script coordinator and the continuity assistant asked at exactly the same time.

The prep tech, who Blythe had always thought looked like an older Lindsay Lohan, took her time while she studied Ethan again. "I've never seen him before. He's definitely never been anybody's guard on my sets. I would've noticed a man who looked like that. No question. Holy moly, is he hot! Has he ever been in the business?"

"Um, no." Blythe had to say something to make all the speculation stop. "I don't think so. I understand he recently left the U.S. Secret Service. The president's detail."

"Really…" It was the script coordinator, whose name on the set ID tag she wore said Amber Sugarman, who seemed most curious. "My cousin is an administrative assistant in human resources at the Service. She went over there from Treasury right before the changeover to Homeland took place. She says all the guys on the president's detail are a big flippin' deal. Why'd he quit?"

Blythe shrugged. "I have no idea."

But her gaze swung naturally in his direction as she said it—just in time to see him bend over to pick up a wayward piece of paper. To her utter humiliation, she found herself secretly checking out the view of him from behind.

"Hmm," Amber began thoughtfully. "Maybe I'll e-mail my cousin and see what she knows about him."

Blythe couldn't think of anything to say. All of a sudden she wanted nothing more than to find out about Ethan's background herself. Afraid to appear too curious around these women she didn't know very well, Blythe casually tilted her head in an I-don't-care manner.

She even managed a laugh, but it sounded hollow to her ears. "Not sure he's worth *that* much trouble. But if you find out anything terribly interesting, let me know. Ashley is my responsibility, after all. I guess it would be nice if I knew more about the people she's working with."

Amber looked down her nose at Blythe, though she probably stood two inches shorter. "Oh, sure. You don't think he's hot at all? Ha! Come off it, girl. Anybody would have to be dead and buried not to go panting after that dude. And you get to work with him all the time."

The conversation came to an abrupt halt as the set coordinator buzzed all assistants back to work. Cell phones magically disappeared and plastic coffee cups and leftover almond danishes got pitched into trash cans as everyone went their own ways.

Actual filming wouldn't start for another half hour, but Blythe had no intention of hanging around until Ashley was called. She really wasn't interested in spending time alone with Ethan—not now or in the future. Not with the way he was forever staring at her. And the way his gaze made her body turn all itchy and tense. It was bad enough that every time she turned around he was always right there.

So let him be the bodyguard. "Ethan," she called out. "I'm going over to Ashley's trailer to work on schedules. Think you can take over the job of making sure she's back on the set when the director calls for her?"

"I suppose I can manage," he answered wryly and with a big wink.

Damn man. He could charm the panties off the nuns. Waving a hand in acknowledgment but afraid to open her mouth for fear of what might come out, Blythe turned around—and ran.

At the end of the shooting day, Ethan pushed out ahead of Ashley but kept her in the protective circle of one arm as he guided her toward their waiting limo. Blythe walked beside him, chin down and with her computer case held in front of her chest like a shield. Meanwhile, a small group of young girls waited at the nearby gate, autograph books waving in their hands as they screamed Ashley's name.

He'd decided the series television business was damned hard work. Hours and hours of hanging around being bored, punctuated by a few minutes of pure terror when the cameras rolled. How could a seven-year-old be expected to put up with such crap day after day?

At least tomorrow was the last day of shooting for this season. Ashley would have to survive it for only twenty-four more hours.

By the time they arrived at the limo, Ashley was dragging.

He literally had to pick the child up off her feet and place her on the backseat. Then he stood aside to let Blythe enter.

Instead of climbing inside, she leaned in to talk to Ashley. Ethan didn't mind the wait. The view of Blythe's backside kept him pleasantly occupied.

At first glance, he'd thought the woman a little too well rounded for his taste. But with another look, he found himself paralyzed, caught in the pure fascination of watching the way her buttocks tightened under her jeans. His imagination quickly took him to a quiet place where he could wrap his hands around all that fullness. If things went his way from there, next he would lift his hands slowly to her breasts, testing and teasing the ripe flesh under her plain beige sweater.

Stumbling back a step, Ethan fought for composure. He hadn't been this turned on by just the sight of a woman's back end since his teenage years. Was he fantasizing only because she seemed so different from his usual type?

Luckily for his equilibrium, Blythe pulled her head out of the car and looked up at him. Their gazes locked, and instead of the cold and self-possessed attitude he usually saw, her eyes danced with the ghost of a smile. A jolt, electric and sharp, smacked him in the gut.

Mercy. Why hadn't he ever before noticed that her eyes were the same color as pale golden tequila with tiny shots of green liquor blended right through the irises?

"I want Ashley to lie down and rest on the way home," Blythe told him. "She's exhausted. I'm going to be finalizing our tour plans with the studio's travel agency on my computer in the front seat. You stay back here with Ash and keep an eye on her."

"Yes, ma'am."

Blythe's eyes changed back to hard, shooting him a

withering look as if to say, *I am the boss, jerk off. And don't you forget it.*

But neither of them was stupid enough to say anything out loud.

Blythe climbed into the front passenger seat, immediately opened her wireless laptop and began to work. Ethan slammed her door hard enough to make a statement, then slid in across from Ashley in back and signaled the driver they were ready to roll.

Five minutes outside the studio gates, they found themselves stuck in bumper-to-bumper traffic. Ethan kept an eye on the cars surrounding them, but he didn't want to appear too nervous for Ashley's sake.

"Looks like it'll be a long ride. Are you going to take a nap like Blythe said?" He'd asked only because as she sat there staring at him, her shoulders were drawn up tight and her mouth had turned down in a frown.

"Only babies take naps. I am not a baby. I'm a star."

Okay, hot stuff. Just what he needed. Another cold, self-possessed female. And this one was only seven. Terrific.

But she didn't resemble a self-possessed star at the moment. As he studied her, Ethan began to see signs of her distress. Her feet absently kicked the seat. She'd slunk down low, fidgeting with her jacket. And her eyelids drooped as though she was fighting to keep them open.

Without giving it much thought, Ethan swung himself around and sat on the long bench beside her. "You know, I have a sister, and you remind me of her when she was your age. Stubborn little one. She'd get herself so wound up that she couldn't sleep at night."

"Where is your sister now?"

"Back home in Texas. She's all grown up. Still stubborn, though."

Ashley continued to stare at him. He'd been using his

lady-killer grin on her, but she never cracked a smile. He spotted the dark circles under her eyes.

"Well now," he hedged. "Maybe you just need the personal Ryan touch. That was the only thing used to help Maggie get to sleep."

The little-girl star narrowed her eyes at him. "What's the personal Ryan touch? Blythe says I shouldn't let anybody touch me unless it's for acting."

"Now, that's real smart, darlin'. You pay attention to Blythe. But I didn't mean a physical touch." He inched away from her on the long, plush seat-bench to make her less nervous. "Why don't you take off your shoes and put your feet up? I'll sit over here and tell you stories about me and Maggie and my brother Josh. That's the way my grandmother used to do for us. If you want, you could put your head down and close your eyes for a few minutes. Not like a nap or anything, mind you. Just so you can listen better."

When she didn't move, he began speaking in as mellow and dull a tone as he could manage. "We were real Texas kids, us Ryans. Texans through and through. Maggie rode a horse before she could walk. And all three of us could shoot and rope and ride bareback by the age of ten."

"Do you still have horses?"

"Sure enough. The ranch back home has plenty of them."

"Uh…Ethan," she began hesitantly. "It wouldn't be like touching if I just used your side to lean against a little while I listen. Would it?"

"No, ma'am. It surely wouldn't." He let loose with another one of his grins, meant to charm her and settle her down.

She frowned, then hiccuped a snort, sliding over beside him as she stretched out and plunked her feet up on the seat. "My acting coach when I was a little girl told me never to overdo it. That's what you do, you know? But keep talking. I'll just close my eyes awhile."

When she was a "little girl"? What was she now? It was bad enough that she sometimes talked like a twenty-year-old. Ethan shook his head at her, but made room.

He felt her relax against his shoulder. "There you go, sweetheart. But what was I overdoing?"

Ashley's eyes closed but she smiled anyway. "I'm an actor. I know acting when I see it. All that grinning and the cowboy stuff. And you do it so well. But that's okay. Just keep talking in your story voice."

Tough little kid, this dainty megastar. Tough and smart. Maybe too smart for her age. Where was the little girl inside there? When did she get a chance to play with friends and just let loose?

Ethan began describing how, as kids, he and Josh had rescued a calf from the creek only to accidentally waltz across the bull's pasture on their way back. Neither one of them had ever run so fast before or after as they had on that occasion. They'd ended up in a tree and had to be rescued themselves.

He hadn't finished his story yet when Ashley's limp body began sliding lower and lower in the seat. She squirmed around with her eyes still closed until she was using his leg as a pillow. Sound asleep. Sweet little one. This quiet, she looked so helpless.

Ever since the Ryan family had been cursed, Ethan had tried not to get too close to any child. He liked them all right, and felt a special affinity toward them. But he didn't want to get too close. His sister Maggie had made that mistake, and it turned her to yearning for something she could never have. The desperate wanting had changed her whole life.

All that wanting wasn't good for a person. Ethan preferred to consider himself rather a lucky cuss to be sterile. One less worry.

But while watching Ashley sleep and keeping one eye out for anything usual around them, he thought maybe this was one kid he wouldn't mind worrying about. One he could get close to for a short while. Just long enough to finish his job.

The next day was the end-of-season cast and crew wrap party. Ethan had never lived through so much air-kissing and fake hugging in his life. He'd always figured politicians in Washington were the biggest phonies on earth. Now he knew better. Hollywood had them beat by a mile.

Ashley had every reason to think the whole world must be acting if they were being nice to you. There didn't seem to be one single down-to-earth person on the entire set.

Blythe headed his way with an offer of a piece of cake, and he had to amend that last thought. She was certainly real and down to earth. Maybe too real for her job?

"We're celebrating," she told him. "The producers just announced the show's been picked up again for next season. Not that there was any doubt. Ashley has made this show number one on the kids' channel. And she draws a great demographic for the sponsors."

"She'll be acting again next year?" Ethan's appetite had just been ruined. It looked as if Ashley might grow all the way to adulthood without ever getting a chance to be a kid.

Blythe frowned up at him. "Of course. Acting and singing are what Ashley does. She loves it. She wouldn't know what to do if she couldn't act."

Of course. Ethan was grateful that the party was almost over. He needed to get away from all the make-believe and go back to real life, where people let kids be kids.

Just as they were leaving the studio that afternoon, Blythe's arm was grabbed from behind. She spun around to find Amber, the script coordinator from yesterday.

"Don't you want to know what I found out about Mr. Yummy before we break for the year?"

Blythe wasn't sure that she did. But she shrugged as though it didn't mean anything.

"Well, FYI, according to my cousin, Ethan Ryan was going places in the Service. Oh, and by the way, he comes from megabucks, too. His folks own that legendary Delgado Ranch in Texas. Oil and cattle, you know? Being rich and on the presidential detail, *plus* the way he looks, made him one of the most sought-after bachelors in D.C."

"Uh-huh." Blythe was now positive she didn't need to know any of this. She turned away, eager to catch up to Ash and Mr. Yummy. Once again, Amber put a hammerlock on her forearm.

"Wait. Here's the interesting part," Amber added coyly. "He left the Service under mysterious circumstances. My cousin heard rumors that he'd been having an affair with one of the women he was in charge of guarding."

Amber took a deep breath, but she was obviously bursting with the need to get the rest of it out of her mouth. "Listen to this. He was supposedly screwing the wife of an ambassador. An older woman. Real old. Maybe thirty-five. Anyway, rumor is the woman broke it off. And then she had to tell his superiors about the affair in order to make him leave her alone."

Blythe didn't think much of that story rang true. What reason would anyone have to push Ethan Ryan away once they had him?

"But that was all just a rumor," she said before thinking. "Right? You don't know if any of it is true."

Amber raised her eyebrows and smiled like a cat, all cannily feline. "I get that you're more interested in the guy than you let on. But remember, he must've left the Service for some reason. In my opinion, the story just makes him seem more interesting."

Right. "I have got to go now. Have a great off-season." Blythe took off at a run, catching up to Ash. She would rather not think about the story being true. It didn't make any real difference. Ethan was just a coworker. Ashley's bodyguard. Nothing more.

She found Ethan and Ash about to run the gauntlet of reporters and photojournalists waiting right outside at the front gate. The director had invited a few of the season's guest stars to come to the wrap party, and a couple of them were the preteen heartthrobs of the hour. The whole place was in chaos. Screaming, jumping girls. Paparazzi yelling and snapping photos.

Ethan waited for her to arrive. "Is there a way we can avoid the crowd? Crowds are perfect places for stalkers."

"I'd like to say yes. But unfortunately Ashley's publicist is here, and she has insisted Ash stand still for a couple of photo ops. It's part of the job."

He scowled, but then visibly shook off his reservations. "Whatever. How long must Ashley put up with this freak show?"

"Just a few minutes. The studio's PR rep will decide when she can go."

Blythe scanned the crowd, looking for Ash's publicist. Her gaze landed instead on someone she had hoped never to see again in her entire life. Howard Adams. Still as gorgeous, blond and tan as ever. Standing half a head taller than everyone else, he could hardly be missed.

What was he doing here? After last year's trouble, Melissa had used her influence to get him fired, and Blythe had hoped that would be the end of him. So why was he here now, alongside the rest of the paparazzi with cameras slung around his neck? Had some other paper dared to hire the jerk?

Blythe didn't want to even think about Howard, let alone see or speak to him. So she quickly turned Ash over to her publicist and then told Ethan to remain close to Ash but to stay out of the little girl's shots. Finally Blythe slid herself backward into the bulging crowd, hoping to find a way to temporarily get lost.

It was bad enough that she had to put up with Ethan, a man who made her pulse spike and her blood run hot, one more charmer who was all wrong for her. She was definitely not in the mood to face the man who represented the worst of her past mistakes.

Chapter 5

A few hours later, once they'd passed by the new gate guard and come to a stop at the front door, Ethan helped Blythe and Ashley out of the limo. He'd expected Ashley to be exhausted on the ride home again today. Instead she'd been all keyed up, babbling and giggling about posing for pictures with the teenybopper heartthrobs.

Ethan supposed that simply meant she was all female, which wasn't a bad thing. Still, at the age of seven, he wished for her sake that she had another interest or two. Playacting and teenage crushes didn't make for much of a childhood in his opinion.

The idea of acting brought to mind those photographers and reporters, leering out from behind microphones and camera lenses at his little client. The whole scene had left him uncomfortable. Any one of them could have been a pedophile in disguise, snapping pictures and daydreaming. Disgusting. Ethan wondered if he shouldn't make some kind of security rule having to do with crowds and photo opportunities attended by more than one photographer at a time. His job was to keep Ashley safe, and he couldn't do his job properly if surprise uncontrolled situations kept cropping up.

Just as the three of them stepped inside the mansion's front door, Ashley put a hand out to stop her guardian. "I wanna go talk to Mama, Blythe. I'm gonna tell her about what happened this afternoon at the photo op. She always says for me to be on top of every chance at PR. She'll be pretty proud I got in every shot."

Blythe looked pained. "Not now, Ash. Remember we're leaving for the tour tomorrow. We need to pack. And Max will be coming over in a few minutes to discuss contracts and I won't have the time—"

"But if we're leaving tomorrow, then I especially want to go see her," Ashley interrupted with a whine. "She's my mommy. It's not fair. You're just mean."

Blythe's expression went from pained to something he couldn't read. Ethan's sympathy went to the girl. Why shouldn't she see her mother if she wanted to?

"Ash, believe me," Blythe began, sounding impatient. "You'll be a lot better off if you do as I tell you. Come on, now. Let's go decide what games to pack, and then get started on the wardrobe…."

Ashley's face crumpled, and big fat tears welled in her eyes. She sniffed loudly and one lone drop of wetness rolled down her check.

"Oh, for heaven's sake, no crocodile tears," Blythe snapped as she threw her hands on her hips.

"Hold on." Ethan stepped in between the two females but addressed his comments to Blythe. "Why don't I take Ashley to visit with her mother? Then you and Mrs. Hansen can do most of her packing and Ashley will help you finish when she gets back."

"You don't understand the—"

"Yes!" Ashley said, and jumped in the air. "Oh, thank you, thank you, Ethan. You're the bestest."

Blythe shrugged a shoulder in resignation. "I give up. All right, Ash. Ethan may accompany you to the pool house."

Ashley lifted her beautiful, dainty chin in triumph and swung around, as all the tears amazingly dried up in those huge violet eyes. "Thank you, Blythe," she politely said over her shoulder, and headed for the patio door.

"Stick with her," Blythe murmured to Ethan. "This is against my better judgment. And she might really need you before it's done."

He would've liked to stay put for a moment to ask what Blythe had meant by that last comment. But Ashley was already skipping her way to the back door and he didn't want the child to get too far ahead of him.

A few moments later Ashley went bounding into her mother's sickroom without knocking. Ethan had never met Melissa Davis, but he'd seen pictures of her, a strikingly beautiful blonde. When he followed Ashley across the threshold and then slowed to stand beside the sickroom door to wait for her, he felt stung by how her mother appeared today. She looked emaciated, with hollow cheeks and skin that carried a faintly yellow cast. Her head was wrapped in something ugly and woolly and her eyes were sunk deep inside her head. There couldn't have been a more perfect picture of a dying woman had a movie makeup artist designed the character.

Melissa's dark eyes cut over to him a time or two, but she didn't bother to acknowledge his presence. Instead, she listened patiently as Ashley told her all about the wrap party and about the paparazzi's demands that she have her picture taken standing next to some greasy-looking kid with long hair.

Finally, Ash wound down. She picked up her mother's frail hand and leaned against the bed. "Mommy, Blythe says we're going away on tour tomorrow. But that can't be right. You said I could have time off and that you and me would do regular summer stuff. Like swimming at the beach and going to see the princesses at Disneyland." Ashley's voice had gotten higher and more little-girly sounding with every word.

Melissa pulled her hand from her daughter's. "Would you please listen to yourself? You sound like a baby. What have I always taught you? The career comes first. No matter what. You do want to be a star, don't you?"

Ashley blinked a couple of times and her shoulders slumped as she answered, "Yes, Mommy," in a timid, soft voice.

"Stand up straight, then, Ashley Nicole, and behave like the star that you are. I'm too sick to spend much time with you during the summer anyway. And even if I wasn't, you have a contract with the studio to fulfill.

"No daughter of mine will renege on a contract. Don't even consider it. You'd be blacklisted in the business. And I would look like a fool."

"Yes, Mommy."

"Fine. Now quit whining and act like a young lady who knows what she wants. Go have your dinner and then ask Blythe if your publicist faxed over the list of those appropriate responses to interview questions that you're supposed to memorize before the tour."

"But…but…" The disappointed but knowing look in Ashley's eyes spoke volumes about her ongoing relationship to her mother. "Can I see you tomorrow? To say goodbye before we leave?"

"No chance. Sorry, hon. I'll be sleeping in before my next treatment. But you don't need me to say goodbye. Get on that airplane and go like a big girl."

Ashley nodded her head and bent over to give her mother a kiss. Melissa turned her head at the last second and the little girl's lips barely made contact with her mother's cheek.

"Bye, Mommy." With her head lowered in defeat, Ash turned and left, dragging her feet as she went.

Ethan turned to follow her, but Melissa's voice caught him before he made it out the door. "Mr. Ryan."

He spun back and waited at attention while Melissa lifted herself up on one elbow.

"I expect you to keep my daughter safe. But I also expect you to use a modicum of intelligence. A delicate star like Ashley has no business coming to see a mother who is on her deathbed. The whole experience will leave her so depressed she won't be able to apply herself to her career for days. Worse, it will no doubt show up on her face in photos."

"But, ma'am—"

"No buts," Melissa interrupted. "This was your fault. Don't let her come here again if you value your job. That's all. Now get out there and protect my child."

Ethan quickly caught up to Ashley. The girl's shoulders were still slumped, her chin hitting her chest, and she looked as if she'd lost her best friend—if she'd ever had one. Which he doubted.

Slowing to a stop by the pool, Ashley raised her hands to cover her face. Her shoulders began lifting up and down as she made sad mewling noises. Unlike before when she'd been acting to get what she wanted, this time it was pretty clear her heart was broken.

"Listen, Ash—"

"I want Blythe," she screeched.

He put his arm around her shoulders. "Okay, little one. Take it easy."

"No!" She pulled away. "Not you. I want Blythe."

Instantly Blythe appeared from the house and opened her arms wide as Ashley ran into them. The little girl pressed her face against her guardian's belly and sobbed uncontrollably.

Blythe shot him a quick I-tried-to-tell-you-so glance before she spoke softly in Ashley's ear. Within a few seconds the little star stopped bawling and began taking deep, relaxing breaths. Then Blythe quietly led her back inside the main house.

Ethan took a couple of deep breaths himself before he followed them at a discreet distance. Maybe it was time for him to rethink where all his clients on this job stood in relation to each other. He had a feeling that he'd been dead wrong about a few things. Most especially about Blythe's relationship to Ashley. Like most things in Hollywood, it was not what it seemed.

Blythe eased her way down the wide aisle of the studio's private jet while casting glances toward Ashley, sitting in her seat way up front. When Blythe had left her own place for the bathroom about ten minutes ago, Ash had been happily chatting with one of the young female costars from the movie cast whom she hadn't seen since shooting had ended.

On this first leg of their summer movie tour, everything seemed fresh and exciting for Ash, Blythe knew. The child had not gotten much sleep last night and would no doubt fade late this afternoon. At the moment, though, she still glowed with the excitement of a little girl on a new adventure.

Glad to be out from under Melissa's influence, Blythe gave in to her churning thoughts about the mother and daughter. Perhaps, over the next few weeks of being away from her dying mother, Ashley would feel free enough to come to terms with her grief. And, if they were lucky, maybe Melissa would mellow enough to find a way to tell her daughter goodbye by the time they got back to L.A.

Shaking her head over the slim possibilities, Blythe looked up to discover that the same teenage costar who had been giggling with Ash before now appeared to be fast asleep in a reclining seat about ten rows back. Meanwhile Ash and Ethan had their heads together playing some game on her laptop.

Blythe slid into her own seat behind them and loosely fastened her seat belt. She was close enough to hear what Ash and Ethan were saying, but not close enough for them to realize she was eavesdropping.

It had simply amazed her how well Ashley had taken to Ethan. In the past, the child star had exhibited a special knack for recognizing phonies. Blythe imagined it came from her early acting lessons, and also from watching so many grown-ups in the movie business who were never exactly who they seemed.

Ash had certainly let her distaste be known when it had come to Howard Adams, despite the fact that he'd done everything in his power to charm her. Such a smart kid. Blythe sure wished she'd had half the sense about Howard that Ash had displayed. She could've saved herself a lot of embarrassment.

But surprisingly enough, Ashley really seemed to be enjoying her time around Ethan. Ash's instincts were good, so maybe Blythe should rethink her own shaky opinions about the man.

Was it possible he was a lot more than just a pretty face, a sexy-as-hell body and a load of charm? Blythe decided to spend a little more time with him over the next few days. Give him a chance. She would try listening to discover the true man inside.

Ethan slipped a small silver amulet shaped in the form of a hand from his pocket and then sat patiently, waiting for Ashley to win her game and stop talking.

He'd tried his best last night to convince Max and Blythe to limit Ashley's exposure to the public and the paparazzi until the police got a better handle on the stalker. But with no luck. The child star had commitments. Contracts. Fans who expected to see her in person and in their magazines.

His gut instincts were screaming loud and clear. Evil lurked somewhere out there, just biding its time. And no amount of security on earth could protect the child from it.

Blythe appeared to have convinced herself that they would be leaving the trouble behind in Los Angles. Ethan knew better. This kind of trouble knew no boundaries. In addition to that, Ashley's schedule was common public knowledge. Her fans—and her stalkers—could find her appearance dates posted on her Web site.

An open invitation to disaster.

"Yes!" Ash said, one arm cutting the air as she closed down her game with the other. "I made it to level twenty-six that time. That's the highest I've hit so far. And you only got to ten, Ethan."

She smiled up at him with a grin that was all kid. She'd beat him at the game and was gloating. His heart went out to the child inside, trying to escape the adult world she'd been shoved into all her life.

"That's great, kiddo. I have something for you."

"A present for winning?"

"Not exactly." He handed her the amulet that he'd specially charmed last night and then had strung on a chain for her to wear. "See, it's the Mano Poderosa. The silver has been made into the shape of a hand. The most powerful magical protection around. Each of the five fingers on the hand represents a saint who will take care of you."

"It's magic? I don't believe in magic."

"Sure you do." He helped her put the chain around her neck. "Isn't making movies a lot like magic? Everyone works hard, but the end result turns out looking easy and more like a dream rather than a job. *You* make magic."

"I guess so." Ashley fingered the charm and raised her eyebrows. "Most jewelry is cold on your skin. But not this one. The metal is kind of warm and smooth. I like it.

"And Margo Stevens," she continued, babbling on in the same breath, "that's the movie star I worked with in *Tender Dreams,* told me she wished upon a star once and it came true. That's like magic, isn't it?"

"Yes, it is. But this amulet is much more powerful stuff. I want you to wear it all the time. Under your clothes and even when you take a shower. It'll help me do my job and protect you."

"All right. I will. Can I make a wish on it?"

"Not this one, sugar. I've already made a wish on it. I wished that it would keep you safe. So you don't ever have to worry, even if I'm not right beside you."

Ashley looked up at him curiously. "Do you have any kids, Ethan?"

He wondered where that had come from. "No. No kids."

"Why not?"

Clearing his throat, Ethan took a moment to think. He'd never told anyone about the family curse. But this magical child might be willing to understand where most adults wouldn't even give it a chance.

"If I tell you something, a story, will you promise not to tell anyone else?"

"Sure. Is it about kids?"

"Yes, it is. You see, I come from a family of witches, and—"

"Witches? Like in movies and books?"

"Not really. My mother and grandmother came from Mexico, and all their family are trained in healing."

"Is your mom still in Texas?"

Cripes. How did he talk himself into such a corner so fast? He would rather not have to say this kind of thing to a child whose mother was dying, but he couldn't lie to her.

"No, my mother died a long time ago. But my grandma is still living. And my grandma's mother is still alive, too. Though, actually, I've never met her. She's a black witch, called a *bruja,* who lives deep in Mexico."

Ashley shivered. "Eww. Sounds scary."

"In Mexico there are several kinds of witches. The black and white ones are what you usually find. Most of my family are white witches—the good kind." He took a breath and watched Ash's facial expression, hoping for understanding. "They're called *curanderos* in Mexico, and they help people. Almost like doctors."

"Are you like a doctor?"

"Me? No. I know some magic, but I never took enough lessons as a kid to get really good. On the other hand, my grandma works hard at being just like a doctor down in Mexico."

"What about the story of not having kids?"

Right. Trust a child to keep you on track.

He smiled at Ash. "Okay, here's the story. My brother and sister and I were cursed by the black witch a long time ago. None of us can ever have children, not even if we want them." Which he did not.

"A curse? Cool. Did you do something bad?"

"Well, I hate to say it, but we did, sort of. It's a long story. We helped my dad take my grandmother back to Mexico against her will. That wasn't good. The black witch was furious and now we're paying for it."

"Is your grandma stuck down there? Why don't you fix it? Bring her back."

"She doesn't want to come back anymore. She says she's happy where she is."

"Oh. But then…"

"My grandmother is a *curandera,* a good witch, remember? She's trying to help us remove the curse by getting the black witch to reverse it, but I don't think there's much of a chance. Some things just can't be fixed."

Ashley sat quietly for a few minutes. He could almost see the wheels turning in her mind and wondered if she was thinking about her mother's illness being one of the un-fixable things in life.

"So your brother and sister don't have any children, either?"

Now, wasn't that a rather surprising question for a seven-year-old? "They can't have any of their own, no. But both of them have taken in children who needed a parent."

Ash leaned back and folded her arms over her chest. "So you could do that, too—if you wanted to, I mean. You could take in a kid who needed a parent."

Man, had he ever stepped into that pile of his own making! How could he not have seen this coming a mile away?

"Look, Ash. I wouldn't make much of a dad. I'm not settled and I don't even know what I want to do with my life. Kids need lots of time and love. On top of all that, your whole life revolves around the movies and I don't live in L.A." He put his arm around her and let her lean against his shoulder. "Your mom needs you to stay with her for a while longer. And remember, you have Blythe. I think you two must love each other very much.

"But don't worry, I'll be here to protect you for as long as you need me."

Ashley's lip stuck out in a pout for a second. Then something else must've occurred to her because her whole face brightened.

"What is it, kiddo? Why the smile?"

"Oh, nothing," she said slyly. "I was just thinking about stars and wishes—and maybe a little bit about what magic can do."

Chapter 6

Oh, brother. Listening to Ethan Ryan spout that load of bull about witchcraft and protective charms made it seem utterly impossible to find any truth underneath his words. Blythe sat back in her seat, wondering what on earth he'd been thinking. What could he have hoped to accomplish by telling Ashley such tall tales?

Black witches and curses. Nonsense, and really, what a wild sort of story for him to have made up. His whole family had been bad and therefore cursed and now couldn't have kids? Hmm. It was too weird. Had he somehow foreseen Ashley's need for a father figure and been trying to warn her not to expect too much out of a guy who only temporarily worked in her employ?

Blythe considered it. Ethan and his company had come highly recommended. Well, except for the strange story about why he'd left the Secret Service. But then that had been only rumors. Blythe thought he had done his job quite well so far.

Perhaps he'd begun to care for Ash as more than just a client. Why else would he have bothered making up such outrageous stories for her benefit? Assuming he did like and empathize with Ash, that part was all good. Caring about her as a person instead of a star would make him do a better job of protecting her.

She sighed, annoyed. Blythe just didn't have time to deal with a crazy Ethan Ryan and his even crazier witch stories. However, as Ashley's guardian, she felt it was her job to keep a close eye on what he said and did—regardless of her time constraints.

He was either a sensitive man in a gorgeous body with an overactive imagination who cared about Ash's welfare—or he was just plain nuts.

The next afternoon Blythe and Ethan stood backstage at a multiplex theater in a Philadelphia suburb, watching while Ash sang the theme song from her movie and worked the crowd. Each time she saw Ashley in front of an audience, Blythe was amazed at how much star power the itty-bitty girl had. She strutted and sang with the authority and vocal power of a person twice her age.

Good thing Ash made her fans so happy. And it was also a good thing that the child had become so determined to have a fabulous long-term career in entertainment. Otherwise, their grueling summer schedule would've been one miserable road trip by anyone's book. Blythe had tried her best to schedule a few days off during the forty-five-day journey, but Melissa and the studio kept insisting on more and more publicity stops.

"She's good," Ethan said without taking his gaze off Ashley.

"Yes, she is." Blythe folded her arms and turned to study the man as he did his job and watched Ashley perform.

"It's hard to think of her being only seven," he said almost absently. "But I'm afraid that just makes for a more difficult situation when it comes to the psychology of a pedophile."

Blythe hadn't thought of that angle. "Do you think her stalker followed us all the way across the country?"

Ethan shrugged but still didn't turn to look at her. "There's a chance."

"But what does he want with her?" The idea of Ashley having to face some madman made Blythe sick to her stomach.

"Could be anything. Starting with the same thing that all sickos seem to want from children…." Ethan's words died out and Blythe's imagination unfortunately ran wild. "Or there's a chance someone wants to nab a ransom for big money. Or it could be he's just after fame."

"Fame? I don't understand. How could stalking a child make him famous?"

"Ashley is famous. If she's kidnapped or harmed in any way, it'll be all over the news. And even if this loser gets himself caught, that might be just what he wants. To see his name in print or on the Internet."

"Ugh. That's a nasty thought. How are we going to find this guy and make him go away?"

Ethan shot her a quick glance that was well over-the-top when it came to charming and sympathetic. "Stalking celebrities is a nasty business. And finding the stalker is almost impossible until he does something overt—and dangerous. That's why it would be a whole lot better and easier if Ashley could stay out of the glare of flashing cameras and strobes for a few weeks. At least until we get a better handle on what this guy is after."

Blythe agreed with him, but she had a job to do. And Ashley had a job to do, too. Ashley's job was to promote the movie and her career. And Blythe was stuck making sure it all went smoothly. no matter what the cost to a sweet little girl. Why couldn't charming, sympathetic Ethan see that?

The frustration made her angry. "If you can't do the job of stopping the stalker and protecting her while she does hers, then just say so. I'd be happy to find someone who can."

He swung around, his normal amused and lazy smile gone. "You tell me how you want me to do the job and I'll get it done—even if it involves consulting tarot readers and psychic gurus or any of the other things I've heard you Hollywood types go for. But I still say she'd be safer on a playground somewhere."

Blythe thought so, too. But she couldn't give him the satisfaction of agreeing with him—because it wasn't up to either of them. Nor would she let him get away with spouting that "Hollywood" crap. Not from a guy who claimed to be cursed. "Listen, you—"

Right then Ashley finished her song, the audience went wild with applause and Ethan jogged to her side to escort her off the stage. Blythe began making her way to the food court where Ash and the other stars were going to be greeting the fans, but she was muttering under her breath as she went. Ethan Ryan had not heard the last from her on this subject.

Ethan stayed within inches of Ashley as the horde of mostly young girls tried to surround her. The house security kept a pretty good handle on crowd control as they held everyone back in single-file lines the best they could. One fan at a time got to move forward for an autograph or to receive an Ashley Nicole doll, part of the movie studio's giveaway promotion.

Though the area near Ash and the other stars seemed

orderly enough, when he looked out past the long lines, the entire multiplex teemed in chaos. Ethan didn't like it one bit. Throngs of reporters lurked in the background like turkey vultures waiting for roadkill. Crowds of parents waited impatiently at the edges of lines of screaming children. Off-duty police and private security mingled throughout the crowds waiting for any sign of trouble.

Ashley took it all in like a trooper. She talked to each fan individually. And she smiled that million-wattage grin for any parents with cameras.

All went well until, suddenly, a demonstration, complete with signs and chanting erupted at the edge of the food court.

Ethan leaned over and spoke to the head of the multiplex security force. "What's going on? Is that demonstration approved?"

The uniformed security boss nodded. "They're the animal abuse folks, complaining about someone wearing fur in the movie. The police had no choice. Had to issue them a permit. But the demonstrators were supposed to keep it outside." He motioned to one of his men and began issuing orders to move the group outside the doors.

Then things dissolved from chaos into World War III. Some of the people in the crowd apparently took exception to the demonstrators ignoring their lines. A shoving and screaming match took place as security people tried to clear out the rowdiest people.

The security boss made a command decision. "Move the movie people and all the kids back to the west lobby until we can clear this mess out of here," he shouted to anyone of his people within earshot. Without taking a second breath, he was on his radio calling for police reinforcements and running full out toward the disturbance.

Ethan didn't need to be told twice. Throwing a protective arm around Ashley, he began wading through the crowd and moving her toward relative calm. He was prepared to pick her up bodily and hit the nearest exit if necessary.

"What's the matter, Ethan?" Ash asked as he dragged her along in the circle of his arm. "What's all the screaming about?"

"It doesn't have anything to do with you, sweetheart. They just want you to take a break for a few minutes while the cops clear out a bunch of demonstrators."

"Oh. But. Um…" Her face bunched up with worry and Ashley Nicole Davis, megastar, all of a sudden looked like a scared baby girl. "I need to go to the potty. Bad. Is that okay?"

"Sure." Ethan felt sorry for the child. As if she didn't have enough troubles with her mother, a stalker and the summer schedule from hell—now this.

He moved them along until he found her an out-of-the-way women's restroom, then stood just outside the door and kept an eye on everyone who went in behind her. Worried about her, he couldn't help wanting to spirit her away from this place and get her outside in the sunshine. The hallways were still too crowded with people to suit him.

"Where's Ash?" Blythe, out of breath, came running up beside him.

"She had to go," he explained as he gestured over his shoulder to the restroom.

Blythe gulped in air and stood panting with hands on her knees. Her almost indescribable hair had gone wild in a riot of curls and those exotic hazel eyes were now shooting gold and green sparks. Her normally calm and sober face was rosy with exertion.

A sudden vision of all that hair flowing free and wild as she leaned over his body shocked him with its unwelcome images. Clearly imagining the soft tickle of spun cobweb hair against his bare skin, he was on the verge of a full-blown fantasy of her riding him, both of them lost in the throes of ecstasy. Ethan took a step back and jerked around to face away from the temptation.

Maybe it had been too long since he'd had a woman. But this one was definitely off-limits, and he knew it too well.

Blythe wasn't crazy about talking to the back of Ethan's head. But she had no choice. "The studio rep wants her to stay close." She took a steadying breath. "As soon as the cops clear out the demonstrators and restore calm, Ash has to be back there to pose for publicity stills."

That got his attention. He turned to confront her. "After all she's been through today, you want Ashley to stand in front of cameras and smile?"

Back in control of her breathing, Blythe nearly screamed at him again. No, she personally did not want the little girl to do any of this. But it was her job to see that the child star lived up to the obligations of her contract.

Fury and guilt opened Blythe's mouth and out spilled words she would never have thought to say otherwise. "*I* am the one serious about doing my job. Unlike *you*, who must think telling a child crazy witch stories will win you charm points."

A muscle twitched under Ethan's eye as he set his jaw and narrowed his eyes. "Did Ashley tell you that or were you eavesdropping?" He moved in close.

"My seat was right behind yours. I could not help but overhear." Blythe threw a hand onto one hip and let her face show how indignant she felt. "Besides, everything that concerns Ashley is part of my job."

He squared his shoulders. "Fine. Then hear this. Everything I told Ashley was the absolute truth, whether you choose to believe it or not. I come from a long line of Mexican witches and my family has been cursed." He faced the ladies' room doorway.

"Prove it." Oh, brother, where had that come from? Blythe needed to calm down fast. This outwardly charming man's mind was obviously out of balance and she didn't want to unduly upset him before she could get Ashley and herself far away from him.

"I'm not crazy," he said over his shoulder. "I could show you some of the magic I know, but you'd probably think I was doing simple magician's tricks. Ashley believed me. That's all that's important."

"Oh no, it isn't," Blythe said through gritted teeth. "She's only seven, and she's my responsibility. I think Max and Melissa would be very interested to know they have hired a crazy person to protect Ash. If you can't convince me you're a witch, I'm going to tell them. It's no wonder you lost your previous job." That last line should've remained unsaid, but she was just so furious.

When he spoke, his voice was low, calm and steady. "This isn't the place for us to discuss it. Aren't you going in to check? If you don't, I will."

"Oh God, how long has it been?" Caught in an abrupt awareness of the time, she screamed the words.

"Only minutes," he said.

Oh, cripes. Why was Ashley taking so long?

"Ashley," she cried as she hit the ladies' room door running full out.

Where had her mind been? How could she have stood there arguing with a psycho while heaven only knew what was going on with Ashley? Her baby must've been upset by all the fighting and crowds. And here Blythe was, casually knocking heads with an idiot while Ashley was doing…what?

"Ash?" she called as she entered the bathroom. The word echoed across the stark empty washbasins and through the nearly empty stalls. "Ashley, answer me."

Panic gripped her neck and squeezed the air right out of her lungs. Gasping, Blythe dashed down the aisle of stalls, checking each one that stood open and knocking on the one that was occupied.

An older female voice grumbled something just as the toilet flushed. But when the door opened and an old woman walked out of the stall alone, Blythe's knees buckled.

"Seems like nobody's in here but me." The older black woman used her cane and headed for the washbasin. "What ya screaming for?"

"Did you…did you see Ashley Nicole Davis in here?" Blythe stammered, and reached out for the edge of the nearest sink to keep herself upright.

"Who?"

"The TV star. Seven years old. About chest high with long blond hair and blue eyes."

"Uh-uh." The woman turned on the water faucet. "Oh, wait. Maybe there was a little blond girl leaving with her mother while I was coming in. But I didn't pay them any mind."

Oh. My. God.

"Does she need help?" Ethan swung open the door and stuck his head inside the restroom.

Blythe nearly knocked him down on her way out the door. "Someone took her. She left with a woman."

"*What?* She's not in there?" He grabbed Blythe's arm as she raced past him.

Outside in the crowded west wing again, Blythe checked for Ashley and then spun toward Ethan. "Aren't you listening? Someone got her. Help me. We have to find them."

"How? How did she leave—and when? I was watching the door."

Shaking, Blythe pushed opened the bathroom door

again. "A lady said she saw Ashley going out with a woman she assumed was her mother."

Blythe and Ethan each took a cautious step inside the empty bathroom. "What lady?" he demanded.

"But…she's gone." Blythe dashed around the far side of the restroom sinks and discovered another exit she'd missed before. "Oh no. How are we going to find Ash now?"

Ethan shifted around in one swift movement and bolted out the door. Blythe followed as he stormed along a wide hallway. About twenty feet down he encountered a man with several cameras slung around his neck. Blythe was close enough to hear Ethan question the guy.

"Seen Ashley Nicole?"

The man nodded his head and waved his arm toward the nearest double door to the outside. "On her way out with her mother. I didn't even have time for a good shot."

Blythe grabbed the man's arm. "How do you know it was her mother?"

"Same blond hair." The man pulled his arm out of Blythe's grasp. "Plus the kid said something like 'Pictures later, please. My mom needs me now.'"

Ethan tore out the door.

By the time Blythe caught up with him, Ethan was talking to a teenage boy who was standing on the walkway. "Did you see Ashley Nicole come this way with an older woman?"

"Yeah, man. You missed her." The teenager swung his arm and turned in a wide half circle. "There. In that blue minivan just leaving."

Blythe spotted a light blue van just pulling out of a space. "I see it. What'll we do?"

"You call 9-1-1," Ethan ordered as he dug frantically through his jacket pockets.

"Maybe we can catch them if we run." Blythe was already breathing hard and she hadn't taken a step.

"Call the cops, damn it. Don't tell them it's Ashley. We don't want them to think this is a PR stunt. Just tell them a little girl has been taken."

Blythe pulled her cell phone out of her purse. But as she opened it and began to dial, she was struck dumb by what Ethan was doing. He had a small shiny object in his hand and was rubbing clear gel from a vial over it. His eyes were closed and she could hear him speaking in singsong words, a language that resembled Spanish. But it wasn't, she was almost sure.

She hit 9-1-1 and during the five seconds it took for the operator to answer, she glanced up to see the van slowing to a complete stop right in the middle of the last parking lot row. Ethan must've heard her gasp and looked up, too, because the next thing she knew, he had taken off at a dead run straight toward the van.

Blythe started after him, trying to answer the emergency operator's questions at the same time. She'd given her name and the location of the multiplex when her forward motion brought her to the row where the van had stopped. The driver's door stood wide open and no one seemed to be nearby.

Ethan was close enough to reach out and touch the passenger side. Blythe held her breath while he wrenched open the back door, bent to lean in and then disappeared inside.

Was Ashley in there? Was she okay?

Chapter 7

"Let me out. My seat belt is stuck, Ethan." Ashley held her arms up and waited for him to fix things.

"I know, darlin'. Give me a second and I'll set you free."

He'd known full well her seat belt wouldn't work. Locking it down was a part of the hex he'd put on the minivan. Even if he did say so himself, it had been a stroke of genius to make the van run out of gas and then have all the seat belts lock down. Unfortunately he hadn't counted on the driver not fastening her own seat belt.

But as he reversed the hex and pulled Ash into his arms, he couldn't be too disappointed. His little client was safe and sound. Let the cops go after the kidnapping driver.

Ashley threw her arms around his neck and her legs around his waist. "My mama needs me. But I didn't like the lady she sent to pick me up. I knew you'd come. How'd you find me? Did you use your magic?"

The police sirens sounder closer. "Shush, sweetheart.

Let's not talk about the magic while anyone else is around. Okay?"

Ashley blinked, then grinned. "A secret? Okeydoke."

"Ashley. Baby." Blythe staggered up beside him and drew the little child star out of Ethan's arms and into her own embrace. "Are you all right?"

"Sure, Blythe. Where were you? My mama's really sick and she needs me to come home."

Blythe gulped in air as if she'd been hit. "No, Ash. Your mama *is* sick, but she wants you to stay with me and keep traveling with the promotion tour. What makes you think she wants you to come home now?"

"The lady told me. She said she was mama's new secretary and she was going to take me home."

"Oh God."

Ethan watched Blythe turn pale green with panic and nausea as Ashley explained what had happened. He worried that Blythe might not be able to keep her feet underneath her for much longer.

"Come here, Ash," he said as he took the child back. "We need to talk."

As he held Ashley in one arm, he pulled Blythe to his side with the other, steadying her against him.

"Listen to me," he whispered to Ashley. "You mustn't ever go off with anyone that you don't know. Not for any reason. Not even if they tell you a story about their lost pet—or about your mother—or about anything at all. It's dangerous. Blythe and I will always be close by and we decide where you go. We're the ones in charge. If for any reason you can't find us immediately, then just start yelling for help the next time someone insists you go away with them. I know you can yell real loud. Do it when you need us and we'll hear you. Understand?"

"I guess so. Am I in trouble?" Ashley's expression grew

dark and her mouth turned down. "I'm not scared, 'cause you watch over me. That's right, isn't it?"

"Yeah, baby girl," he said with a sigh. "That's right. But you still need to promise me not to leave ever again without telling me first."

"I promise."

As the police arrived, Ethan turned Ashley over to Blythe, whose color had returned, and then called the limo to come pick them up and take them to the hotel. He didn't care about photos. Ash had had enough excitement for one day.

Blythe seemed ready to give up for the day, too. She readily agreed to let Ethan handle the police while she and Ashley went to the hotel suite. There wasn't much the two of them could do to help out with a police hunt for the woman who'd driven the van.

But after the cops gave up on their futile search and impounded the van, a detective informed him they needed a statement from everyone. Since staying on the tour's schedule meant they were to leave the next morning, Ethan insisted the interviews take place at their hotel later that night.

As tired as he knew she was, Blythe appeared to be holding up well when the detective arrived. She'd had a shower, her hair was pulled back and her eyes were clear and steady.

While the detective asked Ashley a few questions, Ethan sat back, studying Blythe's face and her posture. He saw vulnerability there, but he was pretty sure the detective was missing it. When she spoke to the cop, Blythe sounded cool, sure of both herself and her job. If Ethan hadn't already learned a few things about the woman's personality and habits, he also would have missed the signs of stress.

After the detective ran out of leads and questions for Ash, Blythe insisted the child be put to bed. When she returned to the room, it was Blythe's turn for answers.

"So despite the fact that you yourself went into the restroom looking for Ashley, and despite the fact Mr. Ryan was doing his job right outside the door," the detective said, recapping her answers, "neither of you ever saw this blond woman. Is that what you're saying?"

Blythe's chin came up defiantly. "That's right."

"And you have no idea why she stopped the minivan in the middle of the parking lot instead of racing away, or why Ashley's seat belt might've gotten stuck—temporarily."

Blythe shot Ethan a wary look over the detective's head but didn't let the man catch her at it. "Didn't you tell us that the minivan ran out of gas?" she asked him instead of answering. "Why would I know anything about that? I can't help you."

Ethan felt sure the cop had been fishing. Looking for a connection between someone on Ashley's staff and the kidnapper. But Blythe wasn't biting.

She was simply amazing under pressure. He liked the way she stood up to the cop—almost as much as he'd liked the way she'd stood up to him earlier in the day. He respected that.

He would have to give this whole day a lot of thought. It had turned out that he hadn't credited Blythe with enough strength. Perhaps he'd better start paying more attention. She was a woman with both intelligence and a strong will. Ashley loved her, maybe even more than her own mother. And he figured Ashley was one very smart kid.

Then he remembered the way Ashley had looked up at him, and wanted to amend his last thought. He wasn't the man he'd seen mirrored in the child's eyes. But maybe he should try to be. Losing his job because of lies and deception—and nothing he'd done of his own accord—had been one of the worst experiences of his life. Now he thought it might just have given him a second chance at a whole new existence.

What would it hurt to try to be more of a man of substance? More the man Ashley thought he was…

The police detective cleared his throat and brought Ethan back to the moment. At last the guy seemed ready to give up on his questions. He probably remained unsure about Ethan and Blythe. But before leaving, he explained about the van being a rental and how the rental car company swore they'd filled it up only an hour before it had died in the parking lot. Furthermore, the detective told them that no one at the rental place remembered what the woman who rented the van looked like and that the driver's license she'd shown was a phony. The credit card she'd used turned out to be stolen, too.

"Again," Blythe interjected as the cop took a breath. "None of that has anything to do with us. We can't help you do your job because we don't know any more than what we've already told you. And tomorrow we have a plane to catch."

She sighed and continued, "It's late. So if there's nothing else…"

Despite her false bravado, she was right. If this attempt had been orchestrated by Ashley's stalker from California, the Pennsylvania cops weren't going to be much help. The blond woman had gotten clean away on foot and the local police would probably play hell finding her at this point. If their stalker had been involved somehow in today's attempt, there was no sign of it. Which Ethan thought he'd better consider a little closer when he had a moment.

By an hour after the detective left, Ethan had finalized a deal on the phone with their hotel, getting added security for the night. After readying herself for bed, Blythe returned to the sitting room, awash now in evening light.

She wore a plain blue nightshirt that hung down almost to her knees and her feet were bare. The outfit wasn't the least bit sexy, but his breath quickened at the sight of her, and he couldn't help wondering what she was wearing underneath.

"There's no way anyone can reach Ash up here on the thirty-first floor, is there?" she asked in an offhand way. "I mean, we should not have to worry at least for the rest of tonight. Or…maybe it would be better if I stayed in Ash's room. What do you think?" Her fingers nervously twisted a wayward lock of hair that had curled loose and lay haphazardly against her neck.

In his memory of their time together, Blythe had never looked so unsure of herself. She was exhausted, he knew. The responsibility for Ashley and the tour had begun to weigh heavily on her, and he could see the result in the shadows under her eyes and the uptight way she held her shoulders.

"You don't need to stay in her room. I'll be right here on the couch if she needs anything. Go on to bed."

"Oh. Um…" Blythe looked around the sitting room as though it held some magical answers for her. "Would it be all right if I sat out here with you for a while? I'm not sleepy at all."

Ethan wasn't sure that would be such a good idea. However, she looked so—lost was the only way to describe it. He couldn't send her off alone like that.

"Sure," he told her as he warned himself to be careful. "Come sit on the couch and we'll talk. Would you like a sherry or an after-dinner drink from the minibar?"

She shook her head and sat down, pulling her feet up under her body on the couch. "Just talk, please."

He knew better than this. After his last assignment, he'd sworn never to get too involved with a client. Ethan didn't want to participate in any conversation that would bring the two of them closer or make them more intimate. Still, he didn't want to hurt her feelings. He respected her too much.

Sitting on the couch, too, he turned to face her. "What would you like to talk about?"

She continued twisting her hair. "It was you who did that this afternoon, wasn't it? Your witchcraft stopped the minivan."

"Yes, ma'am. I figured you knew. And I appreciate your silence on the subject with the police."

Her hands fell limply to her lap and her expression said she was perplexed. He'd bet a brand-new Porsche that she was fighting her physical senses, trying not to accept what her own eyes had seen.

"You're welcome," she finally said. "But they wouldn't have believed me anyway."

Blythe looked like she had something more to say but didn't know how to say it. No need to rush her.

After another moment, she added in a whisper, "Thank you. Thank you for saving Ash. If anything happened to her...I just don't know what I'd do."

"Ah. Of course, you're welcome." With sudden insight, he saw that she was blind to the truth of her own feelings. "By the way, she loves you, too, you know."

Blythe began shaking her head in denial, as though she would've insisted that their relationship was just professional. But then she stopped herself and the ghost of a smile lifted her lips.

"I never thought I'd be glad to have a real witch in Ashley's employ, but I'm sure happy to have you around."

"*Brujo.*"

"Excuse me?"

"In Mexico, witchcraft is considered the normal way of the world," he explained. "It isn't thought of as trickery like it is here in the U.S. There, nature and reality mix easily with the supernatural and the religious. Witches are known as *brujos,* or sometimes as *curanderos* if they're trained in saving people's lives through witchcraft."

She leaned her head against the back of the couch and

closed her eyes. "What else can you do? Can you save lives? Can your magic find out who the stalker is?"

It was against his every instinct, but she looked so helpless and tired that he was struck by a protectiveness toward her that he should've ignored. Blythe wasn't his client. She wasn't his responsibility. And she could certainly have him and his family's company dismissed if she wanted to.

But she also clearly needed someone to lean on.

He rested his arm above her head on the couch and urged her to lie back against his shoulder. "Get comfortable, why don't you? Maybe if we talk a little more you'll get sleepy enough to go to bed."

She slid closer and stretched her feet out, keeping her eyes closed the whole time. "You didn't say what else your witchcraft can do."

"It can't find the stalker. That's for sure. Wish it could. And I'm no savior, either. My grandmother and my sister are the *curanderas* in the family. But I have given Ashley a protective charm I made up for her. That should help keep her safe—if we also do our jobs right."

"Hmm. Do you think… Would it be possible to switch the stalker's attention off Ash and on to someone else using witchcraft?"

Blythe's words had slowed and were less distinct now. Her head had begun sleepily nodding up and down. If she'd been wide awake, he would've scolded her for even thinking of taking her little charge's place. The idea of her wanting to become a martyr bothered him. A lot. But for the moment, he wouldn't make a big deal of it.

"No. Sorry. That's not possible. But don't worry. I won't let anything bad happen to Ashley. Or to you. Trust me."

He should've carried her to bed. Keeping her this close while she slept and not allowing himself to touch was becoming problematic. He'd told her to trust him, but he wasn't sure he could trust himself.

Ethan stared out into the darkness of the sitting room and listened to Blythe's deep, slow breathing. She hadn't bargained for witchcraft. And though he might not be what she'd wanted, he was what she'd gotten.

It was a lucky thing, too. Otherwise, Ashley might already be in the hands of the stalker.

Blythe's last remark about taking Ashley's place was still bothering the hell out of him. Yeah, he knew that she loved the little girl and would do everything in her power to keep her safe. That was clear every time she looked at the child.

But Blythe mattered, too. She mattered to *him*.

He was the one who hadn't bargained for that kind of need. Oh, the arousal he felt whenever they were close was a given. And not in the least unusual. She didn't have to be exactly his type for him to want her. But the constant, crashing drumbeat of that desire had begun to surprise him.

What would it hurt if they acted on their obvious attraction? She was single and he was unattached. Of course, he would need to make it clear that he didn't do commitments. But she was smart. If she'd accepted the witchcraft, then she could understand about the curse and how it colored his life.

She had also been battling her attraction to him. He knew it. Had seen it clearly in her body's responses to him. Could he overcome her natural resistance to a temporary fling? Ethan briefly considered using a love spell, but discarded it. Not macho enough and definitely unnecessary.

He could make her want him without using witchcraft of any sort. And why shouldn't he?

They would be terrific together. The only thing he had to be careful about was screwing up this assignment. But he would take his time. Get her used to being treated the way she deserved to be treated. Like a rare and beautiful gift.

The longer Ethan lay there while Blythe slept in his arms, the more he thought about her—and Ashley—and the stalker.

There was something strange about this stalker. His gut told him that this was no regular pedophile or kidnapper. Ethan had told Blythe the other reason a person might stalk a star—for the fame. And that explanation felt right to him now.

So who could gain something from Ashley's misfortunes?

Well, certainly the paparazzi would have a field day with all the stories spinning around the little star's kidnapping, had the real thing been pulled off. Even the TV tabloids would've benefited. But the idea of any of them needing to make up their own news seemed remote.

The studio's publicity machines might think they would benefit from the extra publicity. But that idea was so over-the-top sleazy that Ethan couldn't really picture it.

A mental image of Ashley's bedridden mother sternly telling her daughter the career was everything popped into his mind. Crap, but wasn't that a nasty thought? Melissa Davis seemed to be a driven stage mother—driven enough to use nearly any means. Although, surely even she wouldn't stoop to such lows in order to fling her daughter into the news. Would she?

Well, she had the opportunity and perhaps the motive. It was something to consider.

In a not too distant motel in New Jersey, the shadowy man screeched into his cell phone. "I will not drop off the rest of your money. You didn't do the job I paid you for. Forget it."

Unreasonable fury boiled under the surface of his normally cold exterior. The stupid blonde didn't deserve the money he'd already paid her. No way would he give her another red cent.

"Don't threaten me, bitch," he continued without a breath. "You know what I can do to you." He wasn't worried about her whining. He had information that would keep her quiet for good, and she damned well knew it. No way would he have tried to use her to pick up the kid if he hadn't known she was more afraid of crossing him than she was of the police. After all, he had the pictures of her indiscretion to back up his threats.

She was only one of several people who owed their continued freedom to him keeping his mouth shut. But this incompetent had just managed to ruin everything he'd worked months to accomplish. He was already considering how to anonymously turn over to the L.A. police the photos of her dumping her husband's body.

Hanging up, he dismissed her from his mind for the moment. Damn it all to hell. Now he was going to have to start over again. And after all of his work setting up this fake kidnapping.

With his hands shaking furiously, the irate man popped a couple of his little Red Devil pills and washed them down with a few sips of warm beer.

Smart enough, he knew he could get what he wanted with more hard work. He vowed to keep at it until all of them paid for their sins and he came out on top. Melissa and Max needed to be beaten down. They deserved everything he had planned.

And Blythe… Originally he'd imagined Blythe and Ashley to be merely collateral damage. But Blythe seemed to be aligning herself with that pretty-boy bodyguard Melissa had hired.

To hell with her, then. She was getting in his way again and he would not have it.

More scare tactics were in order. The tension needed to be strung tighter until he could arrange another attempt at Ashley. No sweat. Blythe was so easy to scare.

Another idea came to him. Not a half-bad one, either. This idea would be bound to shake up the calm for a while.

And a while was all he needed to get back on top of his game.

Chapter 8

She'd dreamed of Ethan again last night.

Darn it. Blythe's dreams had plagued her over the last four days. They'd been the only unfortunate constant in the blur of stops since the attempted kidnapping—since the night she'd slept in Ethan's arms.

Charming visions of him came calling on her nightly in deepest shadows, despite her efforts to stop them. Hot, restless dreams stirred her into a frenzy by prominently featuring Ethan's strong arms, those wide hands, that sexy mouth. She experienced every demanding look flaming in the depths of those gorgeous dark eyes as if they were the real thing. Dream Ethan gazed at her—right through her—into her very center until she burned with erotic, lust-filled passion. All for him.

Each time, she awoke panting, and wanting and alone.

Ashley. The stalker. Her job. All of it lost meaning when morning arrived day after day and she found herself still frustratingly alone in bed.

It was important to keep herself steady. To ignore her dreams and not fall head over heels when she knew a relationship with Ethan would never happen.

But…well, it felt as though she'd fallen under some wonderful magical spell. As though Ethan Ryan had surrounded her in an invisible but warm and protective blanket against the cold, stormy night. Whenever he looked at her, she almost believed that she deserved to be happy. Which was a particularly seductive feeling, and one Blythe had never experienced before.

Breathing deep and shaking her head to clear it, Blythe figured she should give herself credit for keeping her baser needs in check by the bright light of day. But her fondest dreams and wildest wishes continued to stalk and capture her within their gossamer webs every night.

She rolled out of bed, trying to blank out last night's dreams and figure out what day it was. Where were they today? Atlanta? If so, tomorrow would bring a short break in Ashley's schedule, a couple of free days when Blythe had planned a surprise visit to Disney World and time off for the travel-weary child.

Sitting at the edge of her bed, Blythe sighed when her cell phone jangled on the bedside table.

"There's been a change in plans." The familiar voice of Ashley's manager, Max Slotsmeyer, broke through her still-fogged mind.

"Max? Why are you calling so early? It's 4:00 a.m. in L.A."

"Yes, and that makes it 7:00 a.m. in Atlanta," Max supplied wearily. "Time enough for you to wake up our girl and get her to the airport for a ten o'clock flight."

"A flight? To where? Why?"

"Back here to L.A. The studio wants her to appear at the Children's Choice Award ceremony tomorrow night.

There's a rehearsal later this evening that Ashley needs to attend."

"You're kidding." Blythe's mind reeled. "They've known about the award show for months and it wasn't important enough to include it in the original schedule. Why…?"

"That was before they knew that Ashley would be winning the Shining New Star award," Max interjected. "The ceremony has now been moved to the top of the studio's schedule. It's a big enough deal for them to fly her home and then return her to the tour before the Dallas stop on Monday."

Furious at how cavalierly the studio would just do away with Ashley's days off, Blythe tried hard to keep her real feelings to herself. "Does Melissa know about the change in schedule?" she asked quietly.

"Oh yes." Max was breathing heavily through the phone and Blythe could picture him chewing on his day-old cigar. "I spoke with her late last night. Melissa is thrilled by the great promotional opportunity."

"I see." Blythe did see how things went with Melissa— clearly. There was no choice. Not for Ashley.

"How's Melissa doing, Max?"

It took a moment for him to answer. "Not well. Not well at all. But she doesn't want Ashley to hear about how badly her condition has deteriorated. It's even possible Melissa may refuse to see Ash while she's at home."

"*What?* She can't do that. Not to her own daughter."

"Yes, she can, Blythe. And if she does, she'll expect you to find a way to explain things to Ashley. That's your job."

No. Blythe had never signed on for anything that would destroy a child in order to please her mother. She'd been preparing herself to deal with Ashley's grief, but this—it was too cruel to contemplate.

"Does Melissa know about the kidnapping attempt?"

Blythe couldn't imagine any mother who wouldn't want to see for herself that her baby was safe and sound.

"I told her," Max explained in practical and increasingly annoyed tones. "But I soft-pedaled the incident to keep Melissa from worrying needlessly. Ashley is fine. None the worse for it. No sense in stirring things up. Not when Melissa has been so adamant about keeping any negative publicity from tainting her daughter's career."

Negative publicity? Was that what Melissa and Max thought of the kidnapping attempt? When someone could have hurt Ash in the process? Blythe had fooled herself into thinking that Max simply had not told Melissa about the kidnapping in order to shelter her from such bad news at this stage in her illness. Now Blythe knew the truth, and it made her stomach roll.

Quietly, she worked to stifle her conflicted emotions and closet her true feelings. Ashley would soon be needing someone to lean on. Maybe desperately. And Blythe wanted very much for that someone to be her. It would do no good to upset the process at this point, to tell a dying Melissa what she thought of her mothering abilities.

"So what happens to Ash's days off?" Ethan felt incredulous. How could these movie people expect a little girl to keep up with such heavy demands?

He had just called for room service when Blythe broke the news that they would be flying to L.A. instead of going to Orlando for the weekend. Knowing better now than to blame Blythe for the change of plans, he watched as she tried to hide her disappointment and hurt.

"Don't mention days off," she said, irritation shouting loud and clear through her voice. "Ash won't be getting a break for another week. Not until the middle of the Texas portion of her tour."

The setting for Ashley's summer movie was Texas, so the promotional tour included spending a couple of weeks doing special dates in Texas. At first, Ethan had been ambivalent about spending so much of their tour time in his home state. Now he figured he should find a way to make the most of it—in order to do something nice for the overworked child.

In the meantime, he vowed to try harder to smooth out Ashley's days. Whatever it took to see that little girl smile, he would make it happen.

"I'm not going to some old party without you, Blythe. No. No. I won't." Ashley's eyes were filling with those big crocodile tears again. Blythe usually managed to get past the whining, but those fake tears always put a lump in her throat.

It had been such a long day already. Now that they were safely back in L.A., Ashley showed signs of crashing into jet lag. As the two of them stood in Blythe's room, the fatigue on the little girl's face caused Blythe some major worry.

"What's the problem?" Ethan came back from arranging for the studio limo to pick them up for the rehearsal and then again for tomorrow night's ceremony. "Whatever's wrong, Ashley, we'll find a way to fix it."

"Blythe says she won't go to the party tomorrow night. Tell her she has to, Ethan."

He turned to Blythe and raised one of those beautiful eyebrows. "I don't understand. If you don't go, who'll take Ashley?"

"You will."

Frowning slightly, Ethan said, "Yes, I'll be with her as a bodyguard. But that's a whole lot different than holding her hand through the ceremony and being there to congratulate her on winning."

"Both of you will just have to make do. Sorry." Blythe

didn't want to discuss any of this with either one of them, and found herself becoming increasingly sorry that she'd slipped and told Ashley so early about not going. She guessed her own fatigue must be showing through. Too late for regrets, though.

Turning and starting for the kitchen, she hoped to make a strategic retreat before things went from bad to worse. She didn't want to go head-to-head with Ethan right now, not when he looked so sharp, so hard and so damned charming.

"Go lie down for a few minutes, Ash," she said over her shoulder. "The limo will arrive in a couple of hours and we'll have to leave for rehearsal. Tomorrow night isn't anything for you to worry about right now."

Ashley began to sniffle and Ethan caught Blythe's arm before she had a chance to disappear. "Hold it." Grasping her tightly, he turned his head to speak to Ash. "Why don't you do as Blythe says and try to sleep for a while, baby girl? Let me talk to Blythe alone for a minute."

Ashley threw her hands on her hips and Blythe again worried that all hell was about to break loose. The child had been so good for so long. But after another moment, Ash nodded to Ethan and plodded out the door with her shoulders slumped and her feet dragging.

Once Ash was out of hearing distance, Ethan loosened his grip on Blythe's arm. "Okay, explain." He took her by the shoulders and turned her to face him. "What's different about this ceremony? Why aren't you going?"

He'd left one hand on her arm, and she felt the tingly awareness running along her veins and into her chest. She didn't want to speak to him right now. And certainly not about this. *Please just let me run and hide.*

Blythe felt the embarrassment of her entire situation as it crawled up her neck and burned in her cheeks while she fought to get words out. "Nothing's different. I never go to ceremonies or studio-sponsored events. Melissa has always been the one to accompany Ashley to these things in the past."

Taking a deep, cleansing breath, Blythe hurried on. "Admittedly, this one will be somewhat different because Melissa won't be there. But Ashley has you. You'll make a big hit when you step out of the limo by her side."

Ethan had a gut feeling Blythe wasn't telling him the whole truth. Something else must lie behind the crimson color of her face and the way she refused to look him in the eye.

He reached out and lifted her chin. "I don't read minds, sweetheart. You're not making sense. You've been easing into Melissa's place as Ashley's guardian for months. Why not this time?"

Funny, but all of a sudden she didn't look ordinary. Not with that rosy color spreading across her face. He couldn't remember why he'd thought she wasn't his type in the first place, because she certainly radiated beauty at the moment.

"If you must know," she began with a grimace, "I don't have anything to wear. You can rent a tux with no problem, but it takes weeks to arrange for a designer gown. Melissa would never allow me or anyone to arrive at Ashley's side looking anything but spectacular."

A dress? That's what this was all about? Ethan tried to keep the grin from spreading across his face.

"As it happens, I own a tux. It's part of the job." He gave himself permission to slide his fingers across her satiny cheek. "Since tux rental isn't a chore I need to do, how about you let me arrange for the gown?"

Her gaze shot up to meet his. "What? Will you do that by witchcraft? Are you going to act as my fairy godmother?"

Sassy. Ethan relaxed into the warmth of her wit and the intimacy of her presence. She reminded him of his mother and sister, only with a zing of sensual recognition that had been washing over him ever since he'd met her.

"Uh, not exactly," he finally managed with a hard swallow. "But I'll handle it. Will you go, then?"

She shrugged one shoulder, ducked her chin out of his grip and looked away. "You sure you want to be seen with me?"

There it was. The real reason for all the hesitation. Somewhere along the line someone had made her feel inadequate. Damn it to hell. Anger surged down his shoulders and into his arms. He felt like punching something. Instead, he shoved his fists into his pockets.

"You'll outshine 'em all, darlin'." Trying to remain outwardly steady for her benefit, he used his lady-killer grin. "Don't give it a second thought. Just trust me."

She felt like Cinderella. For real.

"You look pretty, Blythe." Ashley twirled daintily around her as they both stared at their images in the full-length mirror in Ash's bedroom.

"Thank you, honey. You look fantastic, too. Just like a princess."

But then, Ashley always looked beautiful. The studio had sent a stylist over today to make sure of it.

It was her own remarkably changed appearance that had been throwing Blythe. She actually did look…special. Pretty, even.

She wasn't sure how Ethan had managed it. But in less than twenty-four hours he'd arranged for the famous designer Iva Swenson to whip up one of her most fabulous and floaty creations, fitting it to Blythe's…um…curves overnight as though it had been designed especially for her. Then late this afternoon Melissa's own hairdresser, Eric, and his entire team had shown up with blow-dryers, straighteners, creams and lotions in abundance.

Maybe Ethan hadn't used witchcraft, but she guessed he had probably bewitched Iva sometime in his past life. Though Blythe would rather not think too much about that. Amazingly all he'd needed to do was say a few words to Max, and Melissa's exclusive salon team had come running.

Ethan Ryan could definitely be a charming devil when he wanted to be.

"Let's go show Mama how beautiful we look," Ashley said as she grabbed Blythe's wrist and tugged her toward the door.

Ashley had thankfully not mentioned going out to visit with her mother since they'd been home from the tour. She'd been much too busy. All that had just changed.

Blythe prayed for some way to save Ashley from having to face a mother who didn't even want to see her. "We don't have time, honey. But your mom will see how good we look on television. Don't worry." Blythe's mind raced to think up other excuses.

Almost as though he'd heard her desperate call for help, Ethan showed at that moment. "Ready to go, ladies? Your carriage awaits." He stepped into the room and suddenly the heat index rose to dramatic heights.

"Wow. Don't you two look…amazing." He gave Ashley a quick grin, then turned his attention to Blythe.

Her knees wobbled. The sensual glint in his eyes made her feel like stammering. Wetness pooled between her legs, and a tiny bead of sweat rolled down the back of her neck. She wasn't sure she could walk straight. Now, wouldn't it be a perfect way to catch his attention if she stumbled and fell down the stairs? Or not. Especially since she was sure it would be so unlike the confident and gorgeous women he usually dated.

Like Blythe, Ashley had apparently been stunned into silence by the sight of him. The child's insistence on visiting her mother seemed completely forgotten. Blythe agreed, the man staring at them looked like Prince Charming.

"Ladies?" Ethan offered each of them an arm and ushered them out the door.

As she negotiated the stairs, Blythe had to force herself to remember he was one of the wealthiest playboy bachelors in America and not really a fantasy prince. She must be more careful—keep her distance—keep her mind on taking care of Ashley.

Sophisticated and seductive beyond anything she'd ever experienced, Ethan would be the sort who enjoyed casual sex and one-night stands, she was positive. And that had never been her style.

Yeah, right. Her *style* usually meant failure. Failure at family. At relationships. At men.

But she wanted to change all that. She wanted to make a go of family with Ashley when the time came. A better family than either one of them had ever known.

Maybe casual sex would be just the thing to turn her life around. Hmm. Not a half-bad idea. Casual sex with Ethan Ryan sounded just right.

If, that is, she could bury her useless standards long enough to figure out a way of getting him into her bed.

Chapter 9

It was all he could do to keep his mind on the job, he'd been so distracted by his hormones lately.

Ethan stood alone backstage, quietly watching as Ashley sang a song and accepted her award and Blythe waited close by in the wings. But he couldn't keep his mind from wandering.

The auditorium had filled early with glitzy, barely dressed twenty-something starlets. But none of them made him look twice.

Not when the sexiest, most desirable body around belonged to Blythe. She might not have their same haughty beauty, but her down-to-earth, voluptuous form turned him on as he hadn't been in—maybe ever.

His tux slacks grew impossibly tighter across the groin every time he glanced at her. A man could get himself lost in those curves. Instead of sensual thoughts of sleek blondes and statuesque redheads, he'd begun to crave only one curvy dishwater brunette.

He tried to make sense of it. Why, suddenly, was it all he could do to keep practical but sexy as hell Blythe Cooper from interfering with his mind, his job, his whole damned life?

Okay, so it'd been a little longer than usual since he'd had a woman. The last six months hadn't been usual in any sense of the word. But he felt sure this sudden overwhelming craving wasn't just about sex.

Or…maybe it was. Maybe he'd developed such a hunger for her exactly because she seemed so out of bounds. If there was a chance to act on his impulses and get the mystery behind him, perhaps this powerful lust would release its hold on him.

"Blythe says I have to go to a press conference now, Ethan. Is that okay?" Ashley's voice coming from right next to him disrupted his mind's fanciful wanderings.

Just in time to get him back on the job. The applause and the sound of the next presenter's voice should have been his first clue that it was time to stop daydreaming. A little belatedly, he set aside the erotic images of him and Blythe and put himself back in the game.

"Sure, honey. Just the way they showed you in rehearsal." He searched over Ash's shoulder for Blythe and found her deep in conversation with one of the studio bigwigs.

Taking Ashley's hand, Ethan walked her down the backstage stairs and into the makeshift press room. Ash wouldn't need a bodyguard to stand beside her as she answered questions. After all, there would be little threat to her safety in such a public forum with studio security checking IDs on everyone allowed backstage. But he didn't like the idea of her being all alone out there facing the hordes of cameras and paparazzi shouting questions.

He stood just out of camera range and watched as

Ashley charmed the room. Ethan needn't have worried. This baby girl was a pro.

In a few minutes several preteens were allowed in to give Ashley armfuls of flowers and presents while the cameras kept rolling. He figured the setup would make for terrific publicity shots and understood why the studio or Ash's publicist might've arranged the scene. But too quickly his little star seemed overwhelmed.

Ethan went to work. He waded into what had turned into too big a crowd and bodily lifted Ash up and away from the screaming girls. As he backed her out of the room, Blythe appeared out of nowhere and took charge of the situation.

He could hear her over his shoulder, thanking the teens and the newspeople and explaining it was past Ashley's bedtime. In a couple of moments, Blythe walked up beside them and reached out for Ashley.

"Blythe, lookit!" Ashley squealed. "My mom sent me a present."

"What?" Blythe took the two-foot-long white box out of Ash's hands. "How do you know it's from your mother?"

Ashley looked perplexed. "'Cause of the girl who gave them to me. She said, 'Your mom told me to give this to you. Congratulations and open it right away for the cameras.' But then Ethan took me away."

Ethan didn't care for the sound of that. "What's in the box?" He took it from Blythe's hand.

"There's a stamp on the outside that says it's the prototype for a new Ashley Nicole doll," Blythe said warily. "But…"

"Oh, goody." Ash clapped her hands and then held them out to Ethan in a movement obviously meant to ask for the box back.

Blythe quickly reached over, capturing both Ashley's hands and her attention. "This might be a bad trick, honey.

The new doll isn't supposed to be ready until fall and the start of your new season. Why don't we—"

"But Mom wouldn't play a trick. My mom loves me. You just don't want me to have anything from her."

Ethan stepped closer to the two females but kept the box out of Ash's reach. "Blythe's right, kiddo. This doesn't seem right. Why would your mother send you a present without mentioning it when she can easily give you stuff any time she wants? If this was really from your mother, Blythe and I would already know about it. Let's go home and check with her first."

Ashley's face scrunched up and Ethan was afraid she might actually break down and cry. And crying would never be on the top ten list of things he wanted to make his clients do.

He took Ash's elbow, spinning both her and Blythe around and marching them toward the artists' entrance. "Come on, baby girl. The limo should be waiting by now. Give me some time to check this box out for curses, okay?"

"Do you really think it might be cursed?" As Ashley raced along beside him, her whole demeanor changed for the better.

He'd been right. Thinking about witchcraft must've seemed a whole lot more interesting and fun for a seven-year-old girl than just being stubborn and teary and wanting her own way.

Thank God.

"Oh, no." Blythe stared down at the poor misshapen form in the doll box and her skin crawled.

Ethan had managed to get Ashley into bed with a promise of talking to her mother first thing in the morning. That and another story about Mexican witchcraft.

Blythe kept getting a sinking feeling that she was

somehow losing Ash's respect and her affections, but there didn't seem to be anything she could do to stop it. The closer they came to the ultimate end for Melissa, the more her control over Ashley seemed to be spinning away.

"Nasty, isn't it? I'm sure glad Ash didn't open this up in front of the press." Ethan held the doll box out for Blythe to see, but he kept it hovering over the kitchen sink as though he thought it might be booby-trapped. A stark-white gift card was pinned to the doll.

The card read *Soon.* In bloodred.

"Why…why would anyone send something like this to a little girl?" Blythe felt shaky. Off balance.

That Ethan stood so close didn't do much to steady her, either. Instead of filling her with warm comfort and a sense of protected safety, his nearness just made her feel more vulnerable and exposed.

Taking another look at the once pretty, blond-haired doll, Blythe cringed at the sight of the mutilation done to the poor thing. One eye had been punched out. A black mark on her face looked just like a bruise. Red markers had been used to make her wrists and feet appear to be bleeding. Her dress was in shreds and her underwear removed. Ugh.

Blythe turned her face and stepped back. What was going on? Who could hate Ashley this much?

"Why?" Trembling, Blythe began almost absently dragging her fingers through her hair. Her designer clothes and all the thick makeup suddenly felt as if they were made of red ants. She wanted this make-believe night to be over. She wanted the memory of it totally erased.

"Easy, darlin'. I'm becoming more and more convinced all of this is only being done for the publicity." Ethan put the top back on the box and set it high on a shelf in the pantry. "I don't think this guy could be a real pedophile or anyone who simply hates the idea of a child star. It doesn't fit the profile. Still, whoever it is seems to be getting more desperate than ever to be noticed."

He came back to her side. "We'll have Mrs. Hansen give the doll to the police tomorrow after we're gone. Maybe they can track down who sent it. When I asked her, Ash didn't remember anything about the girl who handed her the box. I don't believe it would do any good for the police to upset Ashley with more questions."

"No," Blythe admitted. "I agree. I'm starting to think Ash is in much more turmoil than she's letting on. I'm worried about her, and I really wish you hadn't promised she could see her mother in the morning. Melissa has already said she doesn't want Ashley depressed by forcing her to come face-to-face with her mother's demise."

Turning toward the sink, Ethan stared blindly at the darkness out the kitchen windows. "I think Ash is one tough kid. Her mother doesn't give her enough credit. Maybe it would be better…"

He cut himself off, spinning back to Blythe. "Never mind. I'll take care of it. I can put a short spell on Ashley in the morning so she'll forget all about the doll and about my promise that she could see her mother.

"The spell won't last past a day," he continued. "But it should be enough time to get us out of California and back on the tour. Will that fix things?"

Grateful she didn't have to deal with the problems all alone, Blythe stepped closer and kissed his cheek. "No, I should be able to explain things to Ash. It's my job. But thanks for offering."

Realizing her mistake too late, she tried to step back, ducking the fire she'd felt radiating from Ethan. But his hand snaked out and held her fast. The amusement she was used to seeing in his eyes changed to something dark…dangerous…in the blink of an eye.

Every problem she'd thought she had disappeared in a
haze of sensual wanting just that quickly, too. He looked
so good. He even smelled good. What was a woman awash
in this much lust to do?

Trying not to appear so needy that she scared him off,
Blythe closed her eyes and said in a surprisingly steady
voice, "I think I'll go up and get ready for bed. Change my
clothes. Climb into something more comfortable." Oh
Lord, she was babbling.

"Need some help with that?"

Ethan knew he should probably back off and give her
breathing room. It would be the sensible thing to do. But
as her pupils grew wide and dark, and as the flame in her
cheeks ran down her neck and settled in the tender spot at
the base, all the *probablys* and *should've's* in the world
weren't going to save either one of them.

"N-no," she said with an adorable stutter. "I'm not very
high maintenance. I can do it myself…really…I…"

Familiar with high-maintenance females, he agreed
Blythe was anything but. Maybe that's why he'd been
feeling so disjointed around her.

"Oh. You're teasing me, aren't you?"

Yeah, he had been, because he couldn't resist seeing her
blush again. But now that her cheeks had turned pink, he
found he couldn't resist touching. Just for the moment. For
just enough time to run his fingers past the fall of her
cheek. He allowed his thumb to follow that scarlet stain
along the porcelain skin on her jawline and then on down
her exquisite neck.

Ah, but how he would dearly love to tease a sigh from
her throat at this moment. Or maybe a moan of pleasure
from between her parted lips.

But as much as he'd tried to justify a quick roll in the
hay with her, now that it might really take place, he realized

it wouldn't be the right thing to do. She was a long-term-commitment kind of woman. She'd never get involved with any guy who wanted only one night.

Smart Blythe should've been moving back right about now. But she wasn't. She stood there, apparently as stunned by the passion erupting between them as he was.

"Blythe, I…" His throat felt raw, his voice hoarse and rusty. The part of him with the attention span of a golf ball scoffed at his sudden change of heart. It wasn't as though he was afraid of wanting more time with her. Sex was just sex.

He lifted his hand and ran it through his hair. "We…can't." Had he really said that?

She looked startled. As though the sound of his voice had set off some kind of bell in her head. Tipping her head back, she looked torn and vulnerable. But then in the next moment her hand came up to gently touch his face.

"On second thought," she began hesitantly while wetting her lips. "Maybe I do need help with the dress. Come upstairs with me now?"

He took her by the shoulders, ready to shake some sense into her. They couldn't do this. *She* couldn't.

But when he touched the bare skin on her arms, he found her so impossibly hot, so wonderfully soft, that he was lost. A picture formed in his mind of her—wild, with all that mixed-up, curly hair flowing down and raining over his chest. Her face would be filled with ecstasy above him as she squirmed around getting ready to take him in. It was a dream he'd been chasing night after night and now he couldn't walk away from it.

"Ah, hell." He knew when to give up fighting. The desire was too strong to battle.

Slanting a kiss across those plump, wet lips, Ethan lifted her off her feet and headed up the stairs.

At her door, he lifted his head in order to give her one

last chance to stop them from making what might be the biggest mistake of their lives. "You ought to—"

Blythe's gaze met his in a blaze of need. "Just shut up," Her voice sounded as though it were drenched in fire.

Yes, they would no doubt be damned tomorrow. But for tonight, he was damned if he could stop.

Ethan set her down just inside the bedroom door and locked it behind him. The minute her feet touched the solid floor, Blythe wondered if she should stop things. Her brain was backpedaling in fast forward.

But before she could take a breath and decide how on earth to stop, his hands came down, pulled her to his chest and enclosed her in his embrace. Blythe stopped breathing altogether, becoming lost in the notion that her life was about to change forever.

She'd never lost control. Not in her memory. But now she felt crazy with need. She had never wanted…anything or anyone…this much.

No one had ever *made* her want this much.

Ethan apparently lost control of himself, too, because moments later their clothes were torn off in a blur of motion and madness. Her beautiful dress somehow ended up pooled in a heap at her feet. Ethan's tux disappeared into the shadows somewhere.

A few of those movements were lost to her forever. But she fought to keep track of other sensations. There wouldn't be a lot of nights ahead for them. He was a one-night-stand kind of guy and she knew it. This one night was surely all she would get, and she wanted to keep all these wild images in her memory.

Among the things she would remember clearly were the hard angles of his toned and naked body. The wonderfully hot and sleek texture of his tongue as it slid along the sensitive skin of her neck. The prickly way the tips of her breasts smashed against the springy hair on his chest. The musky scent of sex as they both went wonderfully wet with anticipation. The harsh sounds of heavy breathing.

Someone whimpered. That must've been her. Someone cursed. She thought it must be him. Nothing seemed clear anymore save for the erotic madness of this all-encompassing and bruising need.

He brushed his mouth in slow light passes across her breasts, feeding the fire between them. Mouthing one tightened peak, he tormented her by sucking and lathing and nipping in sweet abandon. She squirmed and clutched at his shoulders. In a fury, she reached blindly to touch him everywhere.

His hands went to her hair. Her hands slid down his chest, heading toward his prominent and amazing erection. She wanted to memorize every inch of him before their time was done. She wanted the feel of him against her fingertips to linger forever in her memory. She wanted the echoes of his taste and smell to bring this same frenetic heat to her dreams when she was old and gray.

By now she was damp all over. Bathed in sweat. Washed in fervor.

Remember.

He suddenly yanked down at the scrap of a thong she'd worn under the tight dress, pulling the slinky material lower. She could feel his hot breath as he knelt to slide the impediment along her thighs. She stepped out of the panties, eager to do away with every last material barrier so she could bring him back up into her hands. But he remained where he was. His breath lingered, suspended warm and erotic against her tummy.

Filling his hands with her bottom, he buried his face at her waist. Her knees trembled as she felt his tongue ringing her belly button. Good thing he was holding her tight. Otherwise she would've collapsed on the floor like a puddle of warm Jell-O.

Keep remembering.

His warm and calloused touch against her skin. The way her thudding heart beat inside her chest. His tongue gliding along the tender skin on her lower abdomen, lathing a path of wetness as he headed to— Oh. My. God.

She clearly felt the tip of his tongue probing spots where no man's had gone before. Feel and remember. Nothing like this had happened in her past, and it was unlikely to occur again in her future. She wanted to hang on to every moment in her mind. But things were slipping away fast.

Digging her fingers through his hair, she held on to his head in order to keep herself upright. The zinging drumbeats of his amazing tongue bombarded and tortured her with pleasure beyond anything in her experience. His mouth came down on her again and again with a hunger that in the daylight might have seemed scary. Her eyelids fluttered shut.

He kept drawing her upward toward an elusive edge. Closer to something so sharp it was almost painful. She threw her head back and keened into the darkness.

Suddenly Ethan tumbled them back on her bed. The satiny, cool feel of her silk bedspread added another dimension to the mix as he lifted her hips and pushed himself inside. Wrapping her legs around his waist, she reveled in having him there and pulled him deeper, trying to find that special place where something waited.

Sobbing his name, she clawed at his shoulders. They fused together perfectly. So perfectly, she lost track of where one began and the other stopped. This was a closeness that somehow went beyond two bodies joining in the night. But she didn't know how—or where—or even her own name at the moment.

Deeper he drove, his body now a fiery flame melting her with his brilliant incandescent fire. She arched into him, sobbing and so crazed that she stopped breathing. He whispered erotic words of encouragement against her cheeks as he kissed her tears away. Impossibly gentle and tender at the same time, his body became rock hard as he urged her higher.

And as she climbed, as she sobbed, Blythe lost something more than her control.

Lights exploded behind her eyelids. The fireball roared along her nerve endings as pleasure buzzed loudly in her ears. Shattered and trembling, she clung unsteadily to him as he followed her over the edge. Shouting her name, Ethan's voice sounded shocked at the intensity of his own climax. It gave her a thrill, knowing she'd helped ease his way as he'd done for her.

He rolled with her until her body splayed out on top of his, but he kept them locked together. Both of them lay in the darkness, breathing hard as their heart rates calmed. She knew he felt as sated and satisfied as she did. And maybe he also felt just a little surprised at the power of what they'd experienced.

Blythe was beyond surprised. Stunned was more the word for how she felt.

How could she have let this happen? Somewhere in the middle of the best sex of her life, she had given away her heart.

Chapter 10

Once more Ethan awoke in the darkness, already hard and reaching for Blythe. Was this the third or fourth time that night?

Slanting a glance toward the clock on her nightstand, he was surprised to see it was six thirty. In the morning? He'd never—ever—spent the whole night in any woman's bed. Waking up to the morning light beside a woman you had every intention of walking away from just seemed wrong somehow, and maybe it even verged on being cruel.

Since he didn't do commitment, he didn't do mornings.

Yet here he was—still in Blythe's bed, still hard, still ready to go once again. And he couldn't be too sorry, either. As he lay there, just listening to the soft falls of her steady breathing, he remembered their wild night.

She'd been so tight, so sweet, so hot. He grew sweaty now thinking about it. It had been a night unlike any other. She'd pulled at him, driving him to a height he'd never thought existed. He'd held her as she came apart in his arms, and then she'd cooed and coaxed him until he, too, came—and then came all over again.

They'd been crazy together—insane. They'd laughed. They'd hooted to the stars. They'd even cried.

He'd actually cried at the beauty of seeing her in the throes of ecstasy. She'd touched him in so many ways.

Quietly reaching over now, he snagged one of the soft amber-brown curls that lay upon his pillow. Absently rubbing the satin strand between his thumb and forefinger, he silently ached to touch her everywhere again. His tongue still held her taste. His ears still rang with her languorous sighs.

She had become his weakness. A weakness he really could not afford.

Through the open French door, a staff of light shone against his face, catching his attention and reminding him it was past time to leave her bed. Ashley would be up soon and he didn't want his little client to know he'd spent the night in Blythe's bed.

Preparing to slide out of the room without waking her, Ethan leaned up on one elbow first and looked down on Blythe's sleeping face. How truly beautiful she was. One look and he imagined being inside her all over again. Suddenly hard and panting, he forced himself to turn away.

Maybe there wasn't time enough this morning to snuggle her close and slip inside, but he would give up a year of his life for another opportunity. One more magical night. Or many more magical nights. Whispering a quiet curse at his own foolishness, he realized there would be no chance of even considering such a thing.

As much as taking her over and over, night after night, would make him content, being tied to only one woman simply wasn't who he was. For most of his adult life, he had relished his freedom. Since that time fifteen years ago when he and his brother and sister became cursed, Ethan had made the most of being single. Knowing he couldn't father a child was the excuse he'd needed to play the field and never look back.

A player. That's who he'd always been. It was a self-image he'd cultivated. At least, up until recently.

Somewhere in the middle of their night together, Blythe had made him reconsider his lifestyle. But unfortunately he was too old to shift the course of his life at this stage. Besides, he still couldn't give Blythe or anyone else a child. He had nothing to offer a woman except great nights of sex.

Blythe stretched in her sleep and rubbed against him. The temptation to stay and pleasure her again was pushing him to the limit of his resolve. But he could see no clear way of changing the family curse or his ways. And he understood Blythe well enough by now to know she couldn't change, either. She would never completely comprehend how he could seem to want her so badly and not want to stick around forever. He wasn't sure he totally understood it himself.

Blythe's past had already been colored by someone who had made her feel unwanted. He wasn't sure who or when, but it would kill him to do that to her, too. Even if he hadn't meant to do it. He cautioned himself against being selfish. He had to be a better man.

Somehow he had to get up the courage to leave her bed now for good, and to find a way of making everything between them go back to being simple and easy. For Blythe's sake.

And for his own sanity.

Blythe shut off the water to the shower and wondered what the hell she was going to say to Ethan when she saw him downstairs this morning. He hadn't been in her bed when she'd awoken, and now she was all but panicked over seeing him for the first time since she'd lost her heart.

Stupid woman. She'd actually reached out for him from her sleep—as though he should be there beside her every morning. As though something unusual had happened last night to make him care for her beyond just a one-night stand.

Something unusual *had* happened—to her. She'd had the all-time most spectacular night of her life, and then she'd lost her mind along with her heart.

She knew better. Or should've known better.

But Ethan Ryan was an unusual man. He wasn't like the two men she'd given herself to before. Last night he'd made her feel—oh, my—beautiful. Like one of Ash's fairy princesses. In Blythe's entire lifetime, no one had ever done that. No one had even cared enough to try.

As she toweled dry, a knot formed in Blythe's stomach. Why hadn't she given a thought to the morning after? Even Cinderella had had to face her ugly stepsisters on the morning after her one magical night.

Come on back down to earth, girl, she reminded herself. Your story will not end up happily ever after like Cinderella's.

Cinderella's prince had been charming, all right. But he wasn't a player. He wasn't the all-too-charming Ethan Ryan. Cindy's prince hadn't wanted their magic night to end up as a one-night stand, even though Cinderella had thought that's all it could ever be.

But Ethan had never promised Blythe anything. She had no business expecting anything different than what she'd gotten. One absolutely spectacular, soul-revealing and mind-shattering night where she woke up all alone the next morning. Ethan had probably disappeared from her bed this morning because he hadn't known what to say to her, either. The man was basically good. A decent man who just didn't want to be tied down and who had made that point clear from the start. Her head could understand how he felt, even if her heart really didn't get it.

Unfortunately, by the time Blythe got dressed and entered the kitchen, the knot in her stomach had turned rock hard and had grown to the size of a boulder. She needed to find a way to make this easier on both of them. But how? For their own reasons, each of them needed to get past this one mistake. They must keep working together for Ash's sake.

Hoping she'd learned her lesson, Blythe promised not to let herself tumble for him again. No matter how she secretly wished things could be different. This morning's talk was going to be too difficult to ever contemplate going through again.

"Good morning." Ethan was standing at the sink drinking a glass of orange juice and looking so good that her legs began trembling at the very sight.

"Um. Good morning," she mumbled.

Where was Mrs. Hansen? Why wasn't Ashley downstairs already? Someone should be here to save her from having to face him down all alone. What could the two of them ever say that wouldn't wind up with them hating each other?

"I'm glad we have a moment alone," he said, while staring right through her as though he would rather be running than standing his ground with a smile. "I wanted to say I'm sorry…."

"Sorry for what?" She didn't want him to say that. Didn't want him to ever be sorry for anything where she was concerned.

Her pride kicked her in the pants and pushed the words from her mouth. "For giving me only what I clearly needed? Or maybe for handing me the best night of my entire lifetime without demanding more than I can give?"

She waved her arm casually, as though he shouldn't

think of such a thing. But inside her chest, her heart cried at the forever loss of what they'd shared.

"Don't be sorry for being friend enough to care about what I wanted," she told him while forcing a shaky smile. "Or for being man enough to make sure we get back to a professional level this morning. I can't tell you how happy I am, knowing that we can stay friends, since we'll be working together."

Ethan looked uncomfortable, but he reached over to brush a wayward curl off her forehead. "That wasn't what I was going to say."

"What…what were you sorry for, then?"

He smiled ruefully. "I'm sorry our night is over—and that it can't ever happen again. But I'm glad you do want us to stay friends. You're a special woman, Blythe. Don't ever forget it." His hand lingered against her cheek.

Yeah, right. She backed out of his reach.

"Where's Ash?" she said quickly. "We have a flight to catch and I need to talk to her."

Ethan looked disconcerted at her fast change in topic. "Mrs. Hansen went up to get her dressed a few minutes ago. They'll be back down soon."

"I think I'll go up and head her off at the pass." Blythe spun around, unable to look at him for another minute. "Better get yourself something to eat, Ethan. It'll be a while before we get another chance."

She raced for the stairs. Raced away from the look of pity that was just now appearing on his face. Raced away from the man who thought his poor unwanted lover needed to be reminded of how special she was.

Special? She wasn't feeling it so much. The mountain in her stomach was about to erupt like a volcano, and she didn't want to give him the satisfaction of watching while his new special friend threw up her pride.

* * *

The next afternoon Ethan stood off to the side of the temporary stage set up at the Midland, Texas, mall, watching quietly while Ashley and the other stars of the film finished their songs. As he checked the crowd for any sign of trouble, his gaze landed on Blythe and his mind wandered back to this morning.

It'd been tough, seeing her fresh from her shower, glowing after an all-nighter and looking thoroughly loved. He'd wanted nothing more than to kiss her again. Had even dared to actually touch her soft skin, but not the way he would've wished.

Without trying, he'd opened up his big mouth and hurt her. He'd seen the pain in her eyes when she'd been trying to pretend it didn't matter.

Rubbing absently at the vague ache in his chest, Ethan wondered what had changed. In the past he had never cared one way or the other what happened to the women he'd bedded and left. Life went on. After sex, everyone picked up their lives and put it behind them. Everyone just went on to the next encounter.

Blythe was different.

But why? Why did he care what she was feeling the morning after? And why did he have this sudden need to change his lifestyle?

Was it was because the two of them needed to work together and would see each other every day? That answer didn't feel exactly right. Maybe it was because being around Ashley made him want to step up and be the guy the little star thought he was. But that idea didn't seem to entirely fit what was going on in his head, either.

No, this change seemed to be about Blythe. She'd wowed him this morning as she'd easily handled Ashley's demands to see her mother once before they left town. He had been all set to step in and help Blythe by casting a secret spell. But true to her word, Blythe had talked quietly to Ash for about twenty minutes, telling her mostly just the truth. That her mother was too sick to see her now. And then, amazingly enough, with a kiss and a hug, Ash sort of shrugged it off and went back to packing her video games and books, her demands all but forgotten.

Blythe Cooper would make a terrific mother. She was so good with Ashley. But unfortunately that notion only managed to reinforce what he'd been telling himself all day. She deserved to have her own kids someday. She deserved someone who could give her children and a good life. Someone better than him.

But he was working on it. Oh, not for Blythe's benefit. Any relationship with her was already a lost cause. But for his own sake. By the time this job was over, Ethan wanted to walk away as a man who deserved respect. He might not ever have a family of his own, but he would be a man who could stand tall.

Long after dinner that night, Blythe eased out of Ashley's bedroom in their hotel suite and went to find Ethan. It was late. Ash was asleep. It was time to get this over with. She'd been avoiding talking to Ethan alone all day, but she had to find the courage now to get past that. They had jobs to do.

Rubbing her clammy hands against her pants leg, she drew in a breath but then wished she hadn't. She had washed her hands again and again, all day. She'd taken two showers before they'd left L.A., and another one just a few minutes ago. Still, her skin smelled of him. With every breath she took, and every time she lifted her hands, the scent of him, the citrusy smell of his aftershave and the musky smell of their lovemaking, assaulted her nostrils and made her mind fill with images of them together. Would it never go away?

The magical scent had to be all in her imagination.

Plastering a pleasant look on her face and ignoring everything else, Blythe stepped into the sitting room of the suite. She had to keep reminding herself that being Ashley's guardian was the job she'd been born to do. It was the one thing she excelled at. Nothing else mattered.

"Ethan, may I speak to you a moment?"

He'd had his nose buried in his laptop, probably double-checking their travel itinerary and security. But when he looked up at her with those incredible steel-gray eyes and she got a whiff of his aftershave for real, all her resolve simply vanished. She was momentarily speechless.

Before she totally collapsed at his feet, Blythe managed to plop her body down in a nearby chair. Digging her fingernails into her palms until they burned, she tried to dig up some self-respect at the same time.

Blowing out a breath she hadn't realized she'd been holding, Blythe allowed the burning in her palms to keep her steady and rushed the words out. "I wanted to talk about Ashley's days off. She has several nonscheduled days in a row coming up but I don't want her going back to L.A. Not with her mother's condition.

"You're from Texas originally—where can we go that a seven-year-old would find things to keep busy yet still be able to relax?"

Ethan looked as though he wanted to say something personal but instead said, "I've been giving her vacation some thought already. In fact, I just got an e-mail back from my sister in Zavala Springs. She talked to my father and he's agreed to let us stay in one of his guesthouses on the Delgado Ranch.

"Ash can learn to ride horses and should enjoy the ranch

experience. And though the ranch itself is in a fairly remote part of the country, there are other kids around at my sister's for her to play with. Security should be a breeze."

Blythe's mouth had dropped open in the middle of all that. She closed it, but wondered if the grin on her face would be giving away the fact that she thought he was amazing. Positively amazing.

"It sounds perfect." Could working with him again after last night really be this easy? "But are you sure we won't cause anyone any trouble? Having a TV star around can be pretty intense sometimes."

He grinned. "Trust me, darlin'. No one will treat Ash like a star while she's on the Delgado Ranch. She'll be just like any seven-year-old. And both of you are really going to love most of my family." He said that last with a wink and a lopsided smile. "None of them are anything like me."

Blythe's heart stammered. This side of Ethan was completely unexpected. He obviously loved his family and was proud of them.

She would rather not think too much about him being a family man, though. It would just make her want something from him that he was apparently not prepared to give. At least not to her.

But she would take him up on the offer for Ashley.

That was the important thing. Ashley. Her darling girl and the focus of her job. The job for which Blythe truly thought she had already earned the term *special*.

Several days later, after the last show in Austin, Ethan sweated in the sun as he packed up a rental SUV and prepared to drive himself and Ash and Blythe to Zavala Springs and the Delgado Ranch. The closer the time came for them to leave, though, the more he wasn't so sure this vacation trip had been such a terrific idea.

Of course he'd be happy to see Maggie and Josh, and his new sister-in-law and nephew, Clare and Jimmy. That was a given. But he wasn't particularly looking forward to spending time with his father. A huge gulf still existed between the two of them. A lot of troubled water in their pasts.

However, Ethan had already made the arrangements and now Ashley was looking forward to the trip. So he would go. And he would speak politely to his old man when he saw him, thank him for the use of the guesthouse and throw him a thumbs-up for giving Ash the opportunity to get up close and personal with nature and the animals. And as for the rest of the time they were on the Delgado, Ethan would just stay away from the main house and his father. He would find a way of keeping his mouth shut and his opinions firmly to himself.

See? Already Blythe and Ashley were making a difference in who he was. The old Ethan would never have been able to get within twenty miles of Brody Ryan without telling him off.

Ethan had been surprised a couple of months ago to learn that his sister, Maggie, had maintained a long-term relationship with their father, when he and Josh had blown the old man off and left town long ago. Brody Ryan had deserved their disrespect back then. All of them knew it.

But if this trip worked out okay, Ethan might be forced to admit his father could've changed over the last fifteen years. Maybe.

"Are we ready to leave, Ethan?" Ashley skipped out to the car with her tiny rolling overnighter dragging along behind her. "How long will it take to get there?"

"We'll be there in about four hours, honey girl. Climb on in and when Blythe is ready we'll take off."

As he lifted his little client up into the backseat of the SUV and buckled her in, Ethan couldn't help but hope his father had changed. He wanted more than anything for this trip to be a good one for Ashley. She had so many problems and troubles in her life, and none of them was her fault.

Ash deserved to get away from it all.

Standing in the shadows of the hotel lobby's canopy watching Ethan load the SUV, the secretive man cussed under his breath. "You are not getting away from me, damn it. I won't allow it."

Things had definitely not been going in his favor lately. Everything he'd tried to do to upset Ashley and get things all stirred up had seemingly been brushed under the rug and forgotten. Maybe it was all the new bodyguard's doing, but he doubted it.

No, fortune must be smiling on Ashley. He'd begun believing that some unseen magical hand was ruling his future, though he hated to accept such an idea. But as much as he'd tried, luck had still been with her. Failure and rage were slowly, maddeningly, becoming his constant companions.

Oh, he didn't really want the little girl physically hurt by any of this. She was just the connection he must use in order to take his revenge. The way to get what he needed was through her.

Maybe he should stop worrying about Ashley or any of them.

It might not happen right away, but his time was coming soon. They had to pay. All of them were going to pay.

Chapter 11

"Blythe, look! Cows! Isn't that cool?"

Ethan kept his hands on the wheel but smiled to himself. "Not cows, Ash. Those are steers."

"See their horns?" Blythe also aimed her remark at the little girl, who was sitting in the backseat. "That means they have to be boy cows. Bulls."

"Uh-uh." Ethan softly corrected her. "Not exactly bulls, either. Those are the bachelors who aren't going to get a chance at the ladies." Rather the same as he'd been lately, he thought ruefully.

"The Delgado Ranch keeps the mamas together with their babies," he told them both. "But each of the bulls is kept in a separate pasture. Meanwhile, these steers stay off all by themselves. It makes for a much more peaceful community."

As they'd been driving across the long, empty stretches of range, Ethan surprised himself with how much he remembered about the ranch after all these years away. Just glancing out the windshield at the windblown grasses, the sparse patches of ebonies and mesquites and the miles and miles of prickly pear and yucca had seemed somehow like coming home. He'd been back to Zavala Springs once a couple of months ago when his grandfather Ryan had passed away, but Ethan hadn't bothered to look around then. When he'd left the Delgado fifteen years ago, he had planned on forgetting everything for good.

But having Ashley in the car was making him wonder what it would be like to see things through fresh eyes. A set of unspoiled eyes. Unmarked by hard times past.

Ethan had always wondered why some people badly wanted and needed children in their lives. He'd even asked his baby sister once why she was so determined to either reverse their family curse or find a way around it. Maggie had said that raising babies and growing the next generation gave people the chance to start again. The opportunity to do it right this time.

He hadn't understood it then. But now, showing Ashley the wonders of south Texas and his family's ancestral home, he was beginning to get the picture.

Better yet, concentrating on Ashley kept him from dwelling on Blythe and what their one night had meant to him. Dwelling. Aching. Yearning. All things he could not do. Not and stay away from her as he knew he must.

In fact, right now he was growing tense just trying to ignore her sitting beside him. Maybe he'd be better off if he focused on talking to Ash about the ranch.

"We've been driving next to this barbed-wire fence for a good hour. And you say all this countryside belongs to the Delgado Ranch?" Blythe's sexy voice broke through his concentration, but gave him a perfect opening to go somewhere else in his mind.

"Yeah. For sure." He realized he hadn't thought much

about the ranch's scope and history in years. "Last I knew, the south Texas portion of the ranch stretched out over several hundred thousand acres. There's also Delgado land in west Texas, Mexico and Argentina. But this is where I grew up. This land is my family's heritage."

"Wow. You were lucky to grow up here." Ashley's voice filled with wonder as she gazed out the window.

Had he been lucky? He'd never given it much thought.

"Lots of kids have grown up here," he told her with some pride. "Ever since my great-great-grandfather Delgado received the land as a land grant from the Mexican government. That was back when all this part of Texas belonged to Mexico. Old Don Estaban Delgado found water here. He went back to his hometown in Mexico to buy up all their cattle because the animals had been dying of thirst from a drought. Most of the townspeople came along with the cattle to start new lives here, too.

"That's the way the town of Zavala Springs began," he added. "Those Mexican townspeople needed a place to live while they helped my great-great-grandfather tame this territory and raise his cattle. So he helped them build a town."

"How come your name is Ryan, not Delgado?"

That one was fairly easy—even a little girl could understand. "My grandfather and grandmother Delgado only had one daughter. And she was my mother. She grew up and married a man named Brody Ryan and changed her last name."

"I get it," Ash said thoughtfully. "But not everyone changes their name when they get married, do they? I won't when I grow up."

"That's all right, Ash," Blythe interjected. "I didn't change my name when I was married, either."

"You're married, Blythe?" Ashley voiced the question that came instantly to Ethan's mind.

"I'm not married now, honey. It didn't work out."

Blythe had said that as though it were clear that no marriages ever worked out. Ethan didn't plan on getting married himself, but it still made him curious how she'd become so disillusioned about marriage. He would love to ask her about it. But not just now.

Right now he didn't want to know her any better. Knowing about the ticklish place on the back of her neck and the freckles on the inside of her thigh was already a lot more than he should know.

"Are we gonna meet your daddy when we get to the ranch, Ethan?"

"No, Ash." This explanation would require extra care for a child in Ashley's spot. "Remember about my mother being killed in an airplane accident years ago? Since then, my father…well, he and I don't see eye-to-eye on things. We had an argument back then and haven't spoken to each other in many years."

"My daddy was killed in a car accident," Ashley piped in. "When I was a little kid. And my mommy is dying and can't talk to me much. I guess we're just the same, huh?"

"Not exactly, honey girl. You have Blythe."

In the rearview mirror he saw Ashley break into a wide beam. "Yeah. She's the best."

Ethan heard Blythe's sudden intake of air but knew the sound had been too soft for Ashley to catch. Was that embarrassment he'd heard? Or was she scoffing at the idea of being the best?

He wanted to take Blythe into his arms and make her see that she *was* the best. Damn it. She ought to be able to understand that for herself. Someone should tell her every single day of her life so she wouldn't forget. His fingers itched to glide through her perfect hair so he could point out how wonderful it was. His mouth watered at the thought of kissing her perfect lips while he whispered volumes about how beautiful they were.

She was the best—for Ashley, and for any man with half a brain.

Of course, that eliminated him from the list.

In the rearview mirror, Ethan saw Ash's wide grin quickly turn to a frown as something new occurred to the child. "I have Blythe. Don't you have anybody, Ethan?"

What a sweet girl, worrying about him when her own life was in such chaos. "I have my sister and brother. Wait until you meet them. They're the best, too."

Luckily the town limits of Zavala Springs came into sight. "Here we go. We're almost to my sister's house. We'll be stopping there before we go on to the ranch."

"Is your sister married? Does she have horses at her house?"

"No, Ash. She's not married and the horses are kept out on the range. My sister lives in the town of Zavala Springs and runs the bodyguard business from her home. We'll take you out to see the stock later."

Thank God their seemingly endless journey was almost at an end and he would soon be freed from this luxury prison of leather and lighted dials. Another few minutes of breathing the same air as Blythe without being able to touch her might just ruin every promise he'd made to himself. As big as it was, the front seat of this SUV had become too damned tight for the both of them.

Blythe walked up on the wide porch of the odd old house, stretching her cramped legs and still slightly embarrassed over what Ethan and Ash had been discussing in the SUV.

She loved Ashley with all her heart and had been glad to know the child thought she was *the best*. Blythe nevertheless had wanted to crawl into a hole when the personal discussion had turned her way. No matter what he'd implied, Ethan certainly could *not* think she was anywhere close to being the best. If he had, he would never have been able to walk away from her after only one spectacular night.

Okay, so she knew men were different. They didn't feel emotions such as love as strongly as women did. But still, Ethan had to have been seriously affected by what happened between them. She'd seen it in his eyes. Felt it in the way he'd touched her face and held her hand. And yet he had made it clear there would never be a repeat performance.

Once more in her life, a charming guy had not been what he'd seemed at first. How could she have let that happen?

Sighing, Blythe turned to make sure Ashley was right behind her. One day in the future some woman would settle Ethan Ryan down. He was good with Ashley and would be good with other kids, too—and he had a lot to give a woman. But that woman would not be anyone like Blythe. No, Ethan would eventually lose his heart to someone beautiful and brilliant and probably rich.

"Ethan!" The front door flew open and a pretty young woman who looked a lot like a short, more flamboyant version of Ethan jumped into his arms.

Ethan stood his ground against the onslaught, and even laughed. The sound was good. Sturdy. Masculine. Sexy. Blythe hadn't heard him laugh out loud like that since the night they had made love. It made her heart weep in response. But she kept her mouth shut.

"Oh, wait!" The woman wiggled free of Ethan's arms and bent to throw her arms around Ashley. "Ashley Nicole. What a pleasure to meet you. I'm Ethan's sister, Maggie, and I watch your show all the time. I'm so glad you're our client. We'll keep you safe.

"Hey." Maggie straightened and turned to encompass

them all. "All y'all, come on in." She turned to Blythe and opened her mouth.

"Blythe," Ethan quickly interjected loudly before his sister could say anything else. "Meet my sister, Maggie Ryan. She's a bit…um…eccentric. But we love her anyway.

"Sis…" Turning, he continued with the introductions. "This is Ashley's guardian, Blythe Cooper. She's not eccentric at all. But I think you're going to love her anyway."

Blythe felt a rosy blush rising up her neck. What a strange thing for him to say. Why would he tell his sister she was going to love a perfect stranger when he certainly didn't?

Blythe held out her hand to the young woman, trying to smooth over Ethan's unwarranted enthusiasm. But Maggie ignored the offered handshake and instead enfolded Blythe in a great bear hug.

"Don't stand around on the porch. Come inside," Maggie insisted as she grabbed both Blythe and Ashley by the arms and dragged them along with her through the doorway. "Emma is taking her nap, but she'll be up pretty soon. Wait'll you meet her. What a doll baby. You'll just love her."

"Who's Emma?" Ashley's voice sounded strained, as though she couldn't understand what her ears or eyes had been telling her. Blythe was in the same predicament. All of a sudden she felt as though they'd fallen into a magic looking glass.

Inside the ground floor of the two-story house looked every bit like an enchanted forest. There were plants and candles and statues on every surface she could see. The smell of incense on top of vanilla and something else more earthy and basic assailed her nostrils.

"Um. Nice house. But I'm as confused as Ash. Who is this baby named Emma? Ethan told us you weren't married."

The minute she'd said it, Blythe regretted opening her mouth. Certainly in these modern times a woman could have a child without being married. Blythe herself was planning on being a single mother to Ash when the time came.

But Maggie didn't seem to mind the slip of her tongue. "Naw, I'm not married. And unfortunately Emma isn't mine. She's a four-month-old whose parents were killed in a car accident a couple of months ago. I've taken her in temporarily until we can locate other relatives."

"Oh." Ashley sounded as if she'd been wounded. "Oh. Oh. Oh."

Blythe rushed to Ash and drew the little girl up in her arms. "It's okay, honey. Really. Baby Emma has Maggie until her family can be found—and you have me forever. Everything's okay."

"And both of you have me for protection." Ethan slid over beside Blythe and wrapped his arm around the shaking child. "I'm not going anywhere."

Ashley looked up into Ethan's face with a clear case of hero worship in her eyes. Blythe knew exactly how she felt. She wished with all her heart that they could believe the man. That he really would not go anywhere—ever.

But her practical side knew better. Still, for Ashley's sake, she wouldn't accuse him of lying.

"I'm sorry," Maggie mumbled from behind them. "Did I say something wrong?"

"No," Blythe told her. "It's just that we were talking on the way here about having someone to rely on when your parents are gone. I think Ash was feeling maybe a bit too empathetic toward the baby."

"Oh, sweetheart," Maggie crooned as she patted Ash's back. "Don't you worry your head about Emma. I won't let anything bad happen to her. Cross my heart."

"Ethan said he had you—'cause his mama died and his daddy won't talk to him." Ashley seemed fascinated by Ethan's sister. "He said you and his brother are the best."

"He did, did he?" Maggie pinched her brother's arm. "Well, we think he's pretty terrific, too. Except right now, when he looks like a weirdo in those city slacks.

"Why don't you go out to the truck and get the luggage, brother? Then take it upstairs and change into your jeans. I think all y'all ought to stay the night and go out to the guesthouse in the morning." When Ethan didn't move, Maggie added, "The three of us females will be just fine getting to know each other while you're busy."

Ethan scowled but finally swatted Maggie on the rear end and turned to head out the front door. "Great. By the way, is Josh around?"

"He'll be by later. Josh just got back from Dallas after finishing that weekend security job for the ambassador's son we lined up for him. He wanted to check on his horses at home before he came over."

"Horses?" Ashley's ears perked up.

"You'll see them tomorrow, little bit." Ethan said that with a twinkle in his eye. "I won't be long. I'll just be upstairs stashing your overnighters. Meanwhile, have Mags feed you. You've got to be starving."

"Does she have chocolate chip cookies?"

"You bet I do, squirt," Maggie told her as she took her by the hand. "Let's you and me and Blythe check the fridge to see if I have any milk to go with them."

A few minutes later Ashley was sitting on a big dictionary at the kitchen table, her mouth stuffed with cookies and a cold glass of milk in her hand. Blythe's heart filled with love for the child who had such trouble in her life yet still worried so much about others.

"Maggie," Ashley said with crumbs flying everywhere. "Are you a witch like Ethan?"

"Ashley! That's not very nice." Blythe handed her a napkin, then picked up a wet rag and wiped up the crumbs.

"No. It's okay," Maggie said with a grin that looked every bit like Ethan's. "I don't mind at all. I sure am a witch, sugar. But I'm better at it than Ethan is. I can make people feel well when they're sick. I took special lessons from my *abuela*."

"What's an *abuela?*"

"It means grandmother. Our *Abuela* Lupe is a *curandera,* a healer in Mexico, and was one even when she married our grandfather Delgado. As we got old enough, she taught all of us about the witchcraft. But only *I* got the special healing lessons."

"Ethan told me about his grandmother, the good witch. How'd your *abuela* learn?"

"Her whole family in Mexico are witches. Have been for generations. Witchcraft is a big part of our family heritage. It's kinda cool, don't you think?"

"Yeah!"

Blythe had a feeling that everything here seemed cool to Ashley. But she wasn't positive about how much to let Ash get involved with this witchcraft idea. Taking the girl's red-haired Disney princess doll out of her purse, Blythe handed it over.

"Here, Ash. Play with Ariel. I want to talk to Maggie for a few minutes."

"Okeydoke."

Blythe stepped across the wood-plank floorboards to the other side of the kitchen to stand next to Maggie. Ash shouldn't be able to hear them from here. Besides, the little star already seemed lost in her make-believe world with her doll.

Blythe turned to their vibrant hostess. Maggie's spark-
ling green eyes, gazing out at her from under burnished
auburn bangs, fascinated Blythe. The shorter young
woman reminded her of a pixie. Full of life. Full of magic.

"I, uh, wanted to ask you about curses," Blythe began.

Maggie's eyebrows rose as she checked Blythe from
head to toe. "Are you unwell? What's the matter?" Those
green eyes searched Blythe's face. "Oh, I see. You're in
love. *Unhappily* in love. With Ethan?"

"*What?* No." Blythe lifted her chin defiantly for a
moment, but then gave in. "Maybe. Yes. All right. But that
isn't what I wanted to talk about." She'd wanted to discuss
Ashley's problems, but now all her thoughts were suddenly
centered back on Ethan.

"Oh yes, it is," Maggie corrected her. "Our family's
curse has made a huge difference in all our lives. My
brother Josh has found happiness finally, despite the curse.
He's found himself a love—a woman who's one special
lady and who already has a child. Ethan and I should be
so lucky in our lives, though we probably won't be. I'm
really sorry you've fallen in love with my brother. I'm
afraid Ethan will never stop seeing himself as anything but
single." She put her hand out and patted Blythe's shoulder.

Yeah, Blythe knew that for a fact already. The man would
so rather play the field than settle down, even for love.

Blythe could see a kind of pain deep in Maggie's eyes
and wondered if that kind of ache was also hidden behind
Ethan's ever-present grin. "Tell me how your family
managed to become cursed in the first place."

Maggie sighed and took down two coffee mugs. "Want
a cup?" When Blythe nodded, she poured the steaming
liquid. "It started fifteen years ago, when our mother was
killed in an airplane crash. My father was flying the two
of them back from a cattle baron's party in Dallas. They

went every year. But that time the plane went down. My father broke both legs, but my mother died on impact."

"I'm sorry." Blythe covered Maggie's hand with hers.

"Thanks. I still think about my mom every day, but it was a long time ago. The pain is a little easier to take now.

"Anyway, my *Abuela* Lupe was living on the ranch and I think my father expected her to step into my mother's shoes and take care of us. I was only fifteen. Ethan was seventeen and Josh was about to graduate from college. But my grandmother blamed Dad for the accident. Swore he must've been drinking and that he'd murdered her daughter. *Abuela* was grief-stricken—not herself. She couldn't continue with her healing. Couldn't seem to help the things she said to Dad."

"It must have been tough on all of you."

"Yeah, it was. Especially on Dad. No matter that he swore he wasn't drinking, I still believe he blamed himself for the accident. After a few months of listening to *Abuela* berate him, Dad decided she should go back to Mexico to visit with her own mother for a while. He and Josh drove her down there. And when they arrived, her mother, my great-grandmother, was furious with my father. I've never met my great-grandmother, but she's the black witch of the family, and sort of scary, I hear."

Blythe felt a chill ride up her spine, so she folded one arm around her waist to stem the trembling.

"The old lady cursed at him and Josh," Maggie continued. "Said my dad had murdered her grandchild and then banished her child from her own land. And then she swore his children had participated in this foul deed. She shook her fist and actually cursed my father, saying he would never live to see grandchildren of his own."

"Wow." Blythe lifted the coffee cup to her mouth and discovered her hand was shaking. "That's some story.

And I suppose you all have been to the doctor to make sure it's true?"

Maggie nodded. "Yes. Each of us went immediately. Diagnoses were different in all three cases, but every one of us is sterile."

Blythe respected this self-reliant young woman. If she believed and swore it was true the same way her brother had, Blythe felt compelled to accept their story as fact. Just a few days ago, who could've guessed she would come full circle like this and find herself believing in witchcraft and curses?

"I see. And I'm sorry. You three seem to be caught in the middle."

Laughing wryly, Maggie went on. "Worse than that. My *Abuela* Lupe is caught in the middle, too. She never wanted to hurt any of us. Her wicked mother did that by herself. And now *Abuela* won't have a great-grandchild, either."

"Oh dear." Blythe started thinking of Ethan's charming exterior in a whole new way. She wondered if it was all just an act to disguise his pain. "I'm truly sorry. Isn't there anything you can do to reverse the curse?"

"*Abuela* Lupe keeps trying to convince her mother to undo it. The black witch is dying, though, and there might not be enough time."

"So how do you live with it? How do you go on?"

Maggie took her time with the last sip of coffee and then put her cup in the sink. "I spend as much time taking care of children as I can manage. That's also why I've begun concentrating my private investigator's business around guarding children.

"And...I have Emma."

"But Emma's being here is only temporary, right?"

"We'll see." Maggie's eyes clouded over. "I may turn out to be the lucky one. At least I've had time with Emma. Ethan, on the other hand, has buried his need for children.

It's a need our mother instilled in us from the time we were little. It has to do with our history. But Ethan somehow believes he's not meant to be a father. He's convinced that he would end up like our dad, arrogant and way too strict, and any children would grow to hate him.

"That's the real tragedy." Maggie gazed deep into Blythe's eyes, as though she were seeing straight to her heart. "Ethan would make a terrific father. But I think you already know that."

"Yes, I do." Blythe realized she did know that, deep down where instinct met impulse. And the knowledge caused a terrible ache to form in her chest.

Soft cooing sounds erupted from a monitor sitting on the counter nearby.

"Emma's waking up. I'd better go get her. Ethan should be down in a few minutes. By the way, if you don't mind, I'd like to talk to him alone later. About holding his temper when he runs into our father. And, believe me, y'all *will* run into Dad on the Delgado."

Maggie took another quick breath. "Every time the two of them get together they argue. Actually, it's been that way ever since Ethan was a kid, before Mom died. But I believe Ethan and Dad are just too much alike, and I'm hoping your influence will help Ethan see that."

"I wouldn't count on it. I don't think I have a thing to say that would impress Ethan even one bit." No sense crying over reality.

"Now, there's something *you* shouldn't count on. I've seen the way my brother looks at you. And I'd guess he would listen very carefully."

Chapter 12

Maggie grinned and lifted her eyes to the second story above them. "Emma's calling. See y'all in a bit." She spun herself out of the kitchen like a woman on a mission.

Blythe was speechless. Had Maggie really seen something special in Ethan's eyes? Blythe doubted it.

"Blythe?" Ashley's voice drew her attention back to the child sitting at the table.

"Yes, sweetie? How're you doing?"

"I'm all right. But I was wondering… Ethan told us he argued with his father, and Maggie just said the word *argue,* too. I heard her. Do you argue with your parents or your brother and sister? Did you when you were little? I don't know anybody else that does. Just Ethan."

Blythe wondered what else Ashley had heard. But rather than say anything about Ethan to the curious little girl, Blythe chose to go with the real question. Tell Ashley the whole truth.

"My parents never noticed me long enough to argue. And my brother and sister were very special children. Too special to bother arguing with me." Her older brother was a genius and her younger sister was a beauty queen. She could never compete. "Turns out my parents simply didn't care about me one way or the other. That broke my heart for a while, but it stopped when I decided to become your tutor. You made me feel special, Ash."

Ashley reached up and hugged her neck. "You make me feel special, too. But my mommy doesn't. We never argue, either. She just says what I should do."

Blythe blinked back a tear. How could Melissa Davis not have made this wonderful, unique child feel good about herself? In order to learn her lines so well, Ashley must have near genius intelligence. And of course the little girl was pretty enough to be a movie star and have a doll made in her image. So what was Melissa's problem?

Blythe didn't know what to say—a way to let Ash know how wonderful and lovable she really was. So Blythe just clung to the little girl and kissed the top of her head as they stood in Maggie's kitchen.

"Maybe Ethan's father really cares about him and that's why they argue?" Ashley's mind went in a different direction as she pulled out of Blythe's embrace.

"Maybe so, honey. But I think to make Ethan's life easier we should be real good while we're here and not argue, okay?"

"Sure, Blythe. But I care about Ethan a lot. Maybe I should argue with him just so he'll know."

"I don't think that's necessary. I'm sure he knows you care and I'm not so sure he knows his father does. Besides, arguing takes so much energy. Let's save it for having a good time instead."

* * *

Ethan stood just outside the threshold to the kitchen, listening to Blythe and Ashley. He had come downstairs all set to wage a determined battle with his body's responses to Blythe. He'd given himself a good talking to while he'd been upstairs and had decided he was a better man than to let lust get in the way of either doing the job or making a friend. He'd already been screwed out of his career once when a woman he'd been charged with protecting had come to the conclusion that he was interested in her and had made advances—when he wasn't and hadn't. But he also hadn't cared a flip about that female, beyond doing his best to protect her. He did care about Blythe. He cared too much to mess things up just because they'd had one all-consuming night.

A small shot of pain caused him to look down his arm. He found his hands fisted so tightly they were digging into his palms. Damn it. He hadn't meant to eavesdrop, but now that he had, he was simply angry as hell.

How could Blythe's parents have made her feel so inconsequential? And how could anyone think of doing something similar to Ashley? What was the matter with these people?

Here were two fantastically talented and beautiful females who deserved to be cherished and flattered every day. Instead they'd been born into families without the good sense to see what was right under their noses.

Well, he had these two extraordinary beings here on his home turf for most of the next four days. And he was determined to show them how special they both were. Maybe he would get lucky and really make a difference in their lives while he had the chance.

It was purely a shame that he would not be the one to take care of them forever. But he felt positive some other guy would come along and be "that" guy. All Ethan had was a few measly days here on the ranch and then a few more weeks on the job. He would have to make the most of it.

The next morning, after they'd settled their things into the guesthouse, Blythe stood with Ashley, Ethan and Josh, Ethan's brother, in the middle of a fenced paddock. Josh and his family lived in an old homestead situated on a beautiful section of the Delgado Ranch. Ethan had told her that Josh's wife, Clare, was fixing the place up and making it a home.

Blythe and Ashley were both wearing western shirts and hats with the Delgado logo, which they'd been given along with their jeans. Maggie had also managed to round up riding boots for both of them.

It was amazing how kind and solicitous Ethan had been since they'd arrived. His manner was easy and gentle, and he spent all his time trying to please both her and Ashley. It seemed to her as if coming back to the Delgado had changed him and made him gentler.

The morning sun was hot, the sky a cerulean blue. And Ethan Ryan looked so good, Blythe's mouth watered and her palms grew clammy.

He stood tall in the sunshine, next to his brother and the horse Ashley was supposed to ride. Whenever he removed his hat to swipe at the sweat on his forehead, specks of reddish gold shone on the tips of his hair, attesting to the Irish half of his background. He kept throwing secretive glances her way. Glances filled with subtext and easy-to-read desire.

If those glances meant anything, maybe she *would* get a shot at one more night with the man.

"So, Blythe," Josh Ryan, Ethan's older brother, said casually. "You already know how to ride?"

She nodded, but couldn't manage to drag her gaze away

from Ethan. "Um, yes. Horse riding and grooming were just a couple of the many things that genteel young ladies learned where I came from. Along with knowing not to wear white after Labor Day and how to plan a luncheon menu for forty."

Josh chuckled, but his brother's expression grew tight.

"It's been a long while," she added. "I'm probably a little rusty, but I think I can manage to hang on. At least here in the paddock."

"It's called a corral in Texas, sugar, and you'll be fine. You sure you trust me to teach Ash?" The admiration apparent in Ethan's voice affected her almost as much as his casual touches had been doing all morning.

"Yes, certainly. But are you sure it's really safe?"

"Ash is wearing a protective charm I made for her. She'll be fine. I won't let her get hurt."

Blythe trusted him to take care of Ashley. He was really good with the child. However, she didn't trust him when it came to her heart. Both she and Ashley were no doubt going to be devastated when he walked away for good.

But they would live. They would survive and recover. They would go on. And in the meantime, while he was nearby and warm and smiling, she meant to take advantage of every minute of his time.

Ashley was sitting astride a docile mare, gazing down at Ethan as though he ruled the world. Josh had given her the basics of the child's saddle and tack and then fitted her into the stirrups. Now Ethan took over for a lesson in how to hold the reins and sit competently in the saddle. He spoke gently to Ash, and Blythe fell ever more deeply in love with him. Much to her everlasting dismay.

After about a half hour of slow walking in the corral, Ethan announced to Ashley that she was a natural. Blythe mounted another mare that Josh had picked out, and with

Ethan on the back of a sleek black stallion, the three of them rode out across the grassy squares between painted wood fences and then onto the wide-open range.

It was a glorious day. Soft breezes brought the scents of mesquite and sage; she would recognize them anywhere. Off in the distance, the quiet murmurs of cattle grazing wafted along the air currents.

Ethan and Ash rode slightly ahead of Blythe, but she could hear them talking. Actually, Ethan took the lead for most of the conversation. He was teaching Ash about horses. About how to talk to them and how to treat them gently. He gave her lessons in riding on the open range and what natural dangers might crop up in their way. There were rattlesnakes, prairie dog holes and unseen barbed wire to worry about. He was a very competent teacher.

But sometime during the last serene hour, Blythe had acquired a sense that someone was watching them. Could Ash's stalker have followed them or found them here? Blythe was much more concerned over Ashley coming to harm than she was about rattlesnakes. Still, she kept silent about her *feelings*.

Within another half hour, Ethan turned them around and headed back to the corral, saying, "Ash has never ridden this far and it's been a long while for us. If we stay out much longer, we'll all be too sore and stiff to sit down. We can ride again tomorrow."

Blythe felt relieved to be getting off the open range. Her nerves were straining with worry that Ashley was somehow in danger.

"What'll we do this afternoon, Ethan?" Ashley asked.

"Well, little bit, I believe Maggie has something planned. I heard sis talking to her friend Lara next door about taking all her day care kids on a picnic out here on the Delgado. I think she has in mind eating hot dogs and visiting the farmyard animals. Would you like to go, too?"

Ashley's eyes danced in anticipation. "Oh yes. Will there be baby animals? And is Emma going?"

Blythe had already noticed Ashley becoming solicitous of baby Emma. It was good for Ash to spend more time around babies and toddlers, and to learn how to care for them. Ash led such a solitary life, mostly around adults, and Blythe intended to take advantage of the opportunity for her to become comfortable with kids who weren't in the business.

Blythe was especially eager to have Ash see what regular families were like. Nonacting families. It had turned into a great lesson last night when Josh brought over his wife and their toddler son, Jimmy. Ashley had closely observed the interaction between the two parents and the baby. Blythe wanted other opportunities for her to view how more normal families handled their home lives. She wanted Ash to realize her own situation was certainly not the norm.

Ethan continued by telling Ash he thought everyone would go on the picnic, including baby Emma. And he also said that if Ashley went, she would be in charge of watching out for the baby. Ash lit up at the suggestion. She practically bounced in the saddle, she was so thrilled.

When they were within about fifteen minutes of returning to Josh's corral, Blythe noticed a couple of riders heading in their direction. Ethan stiffened and, as hot as it had become, a chill ran down her neck.

"Is that trouble coming?" Blythe asked him.

Ashley raised her chin and peered into the distance. The child looked to Blythe, then slowed and guided her mare closer to Ethan's.

"No trouble," Ethan answered with an edge to his voice. "I guess my father has decided to pay a visit."

"Your father? The owner and boss of this whole ranch? Really?" Blythe was surprised more than anything. "I'd've thought he'd be too busy to ride out on the range for a visit with his son."

"Apparently not." Ethan slowed their horses and brought them to a stop.

The two riders came up and also stopped their horses, but no one dismounted for hugs. It was easy to judge which of the two men was Ethan's dad. That one looked exactly like a slightly older and more rugged version of Ethan. The elder Mr. Ryan also sat in the saddle like a king, all regal and imperial. Blythe swallowed hard and hoped Ashley wouldn't say anything embarrassing.

"Hello, son," Mr. Ryan said.

Ethan nodded to his father as his stallion snorted and pawed the ground, but he didn't speak.

"Maggie told me you were bringing your clients to stay in the guesthouse," Mr. Ryan continued. "Might've been nice if you'd brought them by the house to meet me."

Ethan cleared his throat but Blythe couldn't decide if he was mad or embarrassed. "Dad," Ethan began as he gestured to Ash. "This young lady is my client, Ashley Nicole Davis. Ashley, this is my father, Mr. Ryan."

"How do you do, sir?"

Blythe would have kissed Ash if she could have reached her. Thank goodness for training in basic manners.

Then Ethan swiveled in his saddle to address her. "Blythe, this is my father, Brody Ryan. Dad, Blythe Cooper is Ashley's guardian and my guest."

Blythe hadn't missed the difference in introductions between Ash's and her own, and she was stunned. Good manners dictated that in any introduction the elder or the more important person be addressed first. Blythe would have expected Mr. Ryan to be introduced to her, not the other way around. She mulled over the difference as she sat a little straighter. A little taller.

"Nice to meet y'all." Mr. Ryan studied them from under the brim of his Stetson as he leaned forward in his saddle and let his horse graze. "Ethan, there's something you need to be aware of. A while ago a couple of the hands spotted a four-wheel drive that doesn't belong on the ranch idling out on the top of Brazos Ridge. The men rode over to tell them they were trespassing. When our hands got close enough, they noticed it was just a single guy in the truck, and he had what looked like long-distance binoculars pointed out to where the three of you were riding.

"Whoever it was took off when the hands got close. And the bastard managed to lose them, too." Brody Ryan scowled. "Sorry about the language slip, ma'am. But I guarantee you he's off the Delgado now. We've checked from the air. And he won't be back. We'll make sure of that."

Blythe wiped away a drop of perspiration that had formed at her temple and shivered, even in the high and mounting heat, at the idea of being stalked again. But she clamped her mouth shut instead of screaming.

"The Delgado must be slipping if you can't keep strangers off the land," Ethan said through gritted teeth. "Appreciate the shout-out, Dad. But I can take care of it from here." The stallion jerked his head to complain and Blythe imagined Ethan's mood was rubbing off on his horse.

She could feel the animosity flowing off Ethan in waves.

Still, she felt relieved to know they were getting assistance in their job of protecting Ashley. "Thank you, Mr. Ryan," she said. "I appreciate your hands watching out for us. Ethan does a fantastic job at security, but he can't be everywhere at once."

Ethan bristled, but he stayed silent and perfectly still in his saddle.

"Yes, ma'am," Brody Ryan said with a dead-on copy of Ethan's grin. "Well, he has only to ask and he can have all the help he needs. I've passed the word. Everyone on the Delgado is aware to watch out for y'all."

With that, Ethan pulled up on his horse's reins and sidled his horse away from the crowd. "Let's go," he told her and Ashley. "Otherwise we'll be late for our picnic."

Ashley turned her mare and followed right behind him. Blythe tightened down on her own reins and lingered a moment. "He's a little touchy today, sir," she told Mr. Ryan. "But I know he appreciates the help. We all do. This ranch is really good for Ashley, and I'm so glad you're letting us stay. I don't want her hurt in any way."

Brody Ryan tilted his head toward Ashley. "You've done a fine job with her. Nobody's going to touch so much as a hair while she's on the Delgado. Don't you worry."

"Thank you. It was nice meeting you, Mr. Ryan." She gave her horse a tiny kick so she could follow Ethan, but Mr. Ryan raised his hand as though he had something else to say. She held back and waited.

"You seem to be an expert with children, Ms. Cooper. But I was wondering if you could work some of that same magic on my son. I'd like to talk to him someday without our history getting in the way."

Blythe could feel the blush rushing up her neck. "I don't know what influence I would have over Ethan, sir. He's the one who practices magic…" She hesitated and decided to go another way. "Your son is no child and knows his own mind. But if I find an appropriate opening, I'll say something to him. That's all I can promise."

Brody Ryan tipped his hat. "That's all I can ask."

The minute they slid off their horses back at Josh's corral, Ethan's good mood returned and he began treating both Blythe and Ashley like princesses again. Apparently seeing his father had not changed his attitude about them.

The rest of the day went like a dream. Ashley played with the other kids just as any regular child would. And everyone treated Blythe and the little child star as if they were family. Blythe wondered what it would be like to become a permanent part of this wonderful group, but she refused to dwell on the idea. No sense throwing time away on wishes that would never come true. She knew better.

Everyone had their place in the world. Ethan had already staked his out, and she and Ashley would never be a part of the things he considered his home.

But Blythe had decided to take full advantage of whatever mood it was that was making him so sensitive to their needs. He was back to being the most charming man she had ever encountered, and this time she liked it.

Much later that night Blythe backed out of Ashley's room after putting the tired child down. Her little girl had been so exhausted after the day filled with fun new things that she'd fallen right to sleep without the need for a story or the usual fussing.

Carefully shutting the bedroom door, Blythe stood for a moment while she catalogued her own aches and pains. Suddenly it was all she could do to move. Ethan had been so right about her being out of shape for riding. She wanted to take a couple of aspirins and hit the sack.

Until…she finally turned and saw Ethan standing at the head of the stairs, grinning at her.

"What's so funny? I'm in pain. I feel like I'm a thousand years old."

He sobered and came her way. "I'm not laughing. I was just thinking how truly beautiful you are and it made me smile." Stroking a finger over her cheek, he made one more comment while he gazed into her eyes. "Sweet mercy."

Blythe's first reaction was to put her hand to her straw-matted hair. She certainly did not feel the least bit beautiful at the moment. More like the ugly stepsister with aching muscles and a sunburned nose. Then she gazed deeper into Ethan's eyes and was surprised at the intense feeling…along with lust, so real and urgent it stirred something similar in her belly.

"Come with me," he whispered. "I've got something I want to show you downstairs."

"I…um…don't think I can walk down the stairs at the moment. I was just deciding if I could manage to crawl into my bed across the hall. Everything hurts."

In a move so quick it made her gasp, he stooped and drew her into his arms. "Then what I want you to see is exactly what you need. I'll handle the stairs."

Chapter 13

"Are you by any chance planning on taking advantage of me, cowboy?"

Ethan just grunted as he took the stairs at an easy pace.

"Well, it's not that I don't want you," Blythe said with as much sexy vamp in her voice as she could manage. Though truthfully, she could barely breathe because of the pain. "But I'm afraid I won't be a whole lot of fun. I'll probably fall asleep within seconds."

He reached the bottom of the stairs and headed off down the hall. Kicking open a door, he stormed into a huge bedroom situated at the back of the house. It had soaring beamed ceilings, low lighting and a master bed the size of Texas.

"Oh, it's fantastic. But still…"

Ethan just kept moving. He passed through yet another doorway into one of the largest bathrooms Blythe had ever seen, done completely in antiques. From the cherry wood cabinet with marble counter to the eighteenth-century chandelier, there were candles on every surface.

Soft scents of lavender and chamomile competed with the soft lighting in setting her romantic senses on fire. And then she saw, right in the place of honor, an oversize, claw-foot tub filled with steaming hot water.

A sigh escaped her lips unbidden. Before she could complain, Ethan set her gently on her feet and began un-buttoning her shirt. She clung to him, but hurt too much to do anything to help.

Tipping her head back to study his face, she tried a flirty grin when he slyly glanced into her eyes. He didn't smile back, but there was a bonfire alight in his gaze, a confla-gration that suddenly made Blythe forget all about her pain. The man wanted her badly. In fact, she'd never seen that particular depth of hunger in any man's eyes. It was intoxicating, even in her misery.

In a few seconds her shirt, bra and boots lay on the bathroom floor. Ethan unbuckled her belt and slid her jeans and panties down over her hips and legs. Having a man slowly undress her was an entirely new experience. A sensual one Blythe thought she could get used to.

Standing there bare and sweaty before him, she had the urge to cover herself as he perused every inch of her out-of-shape body. But there was no disappointment or disap-proval in his eyes. No. If anything, he looked as if he wanted to eat her alive. His lips curved in a feral grin that had her throat going dry.

"Mercy, but you're still the prettiest woman I've ever seen naked."

Her bare body was suddenly a mass of quivering needs. Pressing needs. She pushed her hips out, trying a sugges-tive little movement, and nearly got away with it before she felt the deep ache in her upper thighs in response. "Well, thanks but—"

He didn't wait for her to finish the sentence, just picked her up and gently lowered her into the tub. As she sank into the soothing water, Blythe felt her senses soar.

Handing her a glass of chilled white wine, he said, "You soak for a while." Then he inched backward toward the bathroom door. "Just turn the faucet for more hot water."

"You're leaving?" That wasn't want she wanted. She wasn't sure how her muscles would manage but she didn't care. All she wanted was one more shot at Ethan for the night. Was he going to let all these romantic candles, the mood, the wine and that look in his eyes go to waste?

"I added a potion to the water that should help your body recover. Just let it ease you. I'll be back to check on you in a while." With that he disappeared out the door, leaving her breathing deep, feeling her muscles beginning to relax and frustrated as all hell.

Ethan was feeling pretty proud of himself. Well, proud and as horny as he could ever remember.

Back in the guesthouse's kitchen, he was out of breath and hard as a rock. He'd really had the best intentions when he'd started out on this little errand of mercy. Blythe's muscles needed attention and he knew how to help. The candles and the added scents he'd used would help relax her mind and let her body heal faster.

But what about his own mind? Naked, Blythe's body, all pink and delicious looking, had called to something deep and primitive inside him. The mass of honey-brown curls on her head, tumbling down to tease her breasts, and those hazel eyes all soft and feline as they fixed on his, had turned his brain cells to horse droppings. Seeing her that way again had rendered him incapable of remembering why he'd been standing there.

Feeling out of sorts and itchy, he stepped outside the kitchen door into the yard. Taking a deep, cleansing breath, he looked up at the star-studded sky. God, he'd forgotten how big the sky seemed on the ranch in the dead of night. Without city lights, thousands of beams from distant constellations sparked up the sky with lights so clear and close he felt as though he could reach out and touch them.

Yet, as beautiful as the stars were tonight, and as much as they could set him at ease, they didn't come close to making him forget about the sparkle in Blythe's eyes.

He was going to cave. Reason and resolution be damned. It was only a matter of how long he could manage to hold off before he went back into the bathroom and let his hands get lost in that lovely cloud of sexy hair. Until he lost himself entirely in the spark and sizzle that was all Blythe.

Blythe drowsed in the water. Dreamy, lethargic and insubstantial. Steam surrounded her with a hazy fog of lazy lust. She felt boneless—but still needy. Her dreams were all of Ethan. Of what she wanted to do to him, and him to her. She wanted to wind her newly healed limbs around his waist while he drove deep inside her body.

She wanted to—

Through her haze, she heard the bathroom door creak open. She could barely summon the energy to open her eyes, so she left them closed. It was Ethan. She could almost taste him.

Without saying a word, he eased into the tub behind her and pulled her back against his chest. Yes, this was the man she'd been dreaming about. Wanting to hold him. Needing to touch him. Dying for the feel of his strength against her skin.

He ran his warm, broad hands over her flesh, teasing, savoring and exploring. She heard herself whimper, but knew it was more of a demand. He must have known it, too, because he buried his face in her hair and groaned.

Wild, erotic imaginings careened through her brain as he pressed his erection against her back and then palmed his hand between her legs. She erupted with a throaty cry as the shattering quakes began in earnest.

Ethan whispered in her ear. He was pleading for her to end his misery. To take him inside. His words were sexy, coarse and raw. And she loved it.

"Do you feel what happens…in your body…to mine…when I touch you this way? You're killing me here, sugar. Come for me. Let me in."

It gave her power to know she was testing his endurance. She threw her head back and laughed in the face of his erotic misery. Feeling her domination over him as his muscles quivered beneath her, she wanted him to beg. Wanted to feel him go insane with need and know she was the one who caused it.

She rose up and rolled. Their lips met in a mind-melding, bone-shattering kiss that had her heart fluttering wildly inside her chest.

Dazed by a combination of his sedative potion and plain old lusty passion, she eased back and watched him writhe. But Ethan surprised her by dragging them both out of the tub and onto the most luxurious bath mat she'd ever seen. The move awoke a greater passion in her and she urged him to lay back as she took over. The wetness grew thick, both at the juncture of her thighs and at the tip of his erection. Not able to help herself or to keep him waiting any longer, Blythe bent and took the tip of him into her mouth.

Ethan moaned and jerked his hips involuntarily. She would have given him another throaty laugh had she not been so busy tasting, sucking and listening to him go wild. Full of herself and pleased to be torturing him, she licked a path up one side of him and then down the other. She used her hand to stroke and her tongue to tickle, until her mouth opened wide and took him in deep.

"Mercy, but you've got a wicked mouth, darlin'." His breathing turned shallow.

Smiling to herself, she did a few odd maneuvers with her tongue and felt him squirm. Too soon, she knew the quakes of climax were about to overcome her. Her blood boiled as she tried to hold back. Ethan must have sensed her getting close, or maybe he was also too close to wait.

He struggled to lift her head away from him, then helped her drop down on his erection when she came to her knees. Their bodies were slick with water, sweat and anticipation.

As she swiveled her hips and took him deeper, her pulse hammered, all raw and fierce. She nearly went blind when he bent double and tasted each breast. He caught one nipple between his teeth and tugged, and it sent her into complete bliss. Too soon. She wanted more. She wanted to keep this feeling of power and glory going on all night.

He bucked his hips, drove ever deeper and caused the vibrations to move along her spine. The man had some wicked moves of his own. Her belly tightened just as the edge of that elusive but exquisite pain gripped her in its brilliant passion. He moaned and begged, and she heard her own moans coming faster in high-pitched tones that sounded more like screams.

Moving fast, he flipped her onto her back without ever breaking contact. His eyes locked with hers as a wave of desire rolled over them. Pleasure cascaded through her body, swamping her with erotic impulses and making her deaf, dumb and blind to everything else but Ethan. The two of them moved together against the rising tide of sensation.

His name echoed through her head. *Ethan.* Oh, Ethan. Over and over she said it like a prayer. Until finally, on a simultaneous jolt, they rode their final crest into oblivion as one.

Ethan couldn't think too much. Under the circumstances, he decided to simply take what was offered and enjoy.

And enjoy he did. All through that night he held Blythe in his arms while her body recuperated, both from the horseback riding and from the overzealous sex. He watched her while she slept. Then watched as she stretched her body and awoke to greet the morning sun.

There was nothing in his experience to explain how he felt as the two of them went through the next day and the day after that. Showing Blythe and Ashley around the ranch became an eye-opening experience for him. Suddenly, accompanied by these two people he had come to care for, all the old pain of his mother's death and his subsequent hatred of everything to do with the Delgado seemed somehow muted.

The harsh colors in a typical summer's worth of dried vegetation had overnight turned to soft pastels. And the clashing sounds as the ranch hands worked hard in the hot sun and then played just as hard when the sun went down had all but disappeared, leaving only the gentle notes of cattle crooning over the range.

Lazy, enjoyable daylight hours spent riding, talking with and teaching Ashley slipped into less lazy but just as enjoyable nighttime hours spent in bed with Blythe. Riding, talking and learning pleasure.

In the back of his mind, Ethan knew this couldn't last. It was a dream—a vacation from real life. His real life was an endless list of lonely, hard jobs, and being ever mindful of suspicious behavior and betrayals. Eventually, everything would return to the way it was. All of them would go back to work and the Delgado would once again be a place he wanted to leave behind. But for now...

Early on the third morning, Ashley looked up at him as the two of them strolled across his brother's yard and headed for the foaling barn. "Do you think Miss Molly has had her foal yet?"

He shrugged and smiled down at the precocious seven-going-on-thirty-year-old. "Hope so. She's late in delivering."

"Ethan..." Ash dropped her chin and stared at her feet. "Do we really have to leave tomorrow? I love it here. Can't we stay?"

"Now, you know we have to go back to work, little bit. There're people counting on you. You've got at least another two weeks of shows scheduled."

Ashley frowned. "I know. But if they weren't—if I was just a girl, it would be okay if we stayed, wouldn't it? Your daddy wouldn't mind us living here. Maggie said he loves you."

Ethan felt tension beginning to grip his shoulders and deliberately forced them to relax. "My granddad Delgado left part of this ranch in trust to me. I can do anything I want with that part of the land...including live on it. It wouldn't be up to my father."

Ethan swallowed hard and took regular, even breaths so as not to let the child see he'd been upset by the discussion of his father and his heritage. But he was also amazed to find it didn't bother him as much as usual.

"Ash, you know we all have jobs to do. You and me and Blythe. And when this vacation is over, we'll be going right back to doing what we each do best. You love being an actress, don't you?"

Ashley wouldn't look at him, but she nodded her

head. "Sure. But…" Her words trailed off and Ethan's gut churned.

He knew part of her would rather be just a little girl like everyone else. But they both had their life's paths already set out for them. Ash had to be the star she was. And he was destined to go on in his solitary way, guarding and protecting those most vulnerable.

"Look," he began. "There's almost two whole days left to spend here on the Delgado. Let's make the most of them and pretend we never have to leave so we can just lie back and enjoy the ranch. Okay?"

"I guess so."

"Great." He picked up her hand and held it lightly as they continued on their way. "We won't even think about leaving, sugar. We'll be so busy having lots of fun for the next two days it won't matter. I promise."

Well, that was one promise it looked as though he wasn't going to be able to keep.

As he and Blythe were standing just outside Maggie's house later that day, Blythe clicked off her cell phone and shook her head. "That was Max. I guess you figured as much."

Ethan waited for it.

"It's Melissa. The doctors say she hasn't much time left. But she refuses to go to the hospital. Says she wants to die in her own bed. They're moving her back to the house now. And she wants to see Ashley."

Blythe sighed. "I would put this off indefinitely if I could. I hate that Ash has to face her mother's death head-on and so soon. But we've got no choice. We need to leave right away if we're going to make it while Melissa is still conscious enough to know her own daughter. I'll go tell Ash to start packing."

He hooked Blythe by the arm, turned her back and took

her into his arms, holding her still for the moment. The end of their idyll had arrived too soon, and the idea of never having another chance like this was killing him.

Blythe sighed against his chest. "Thanks for being there. These past few days have been…really special for me. And for Ash. I don't know how I'll ever thank you for taking us into your family and showing us such a good time. I…"

She sighed again as he placed a gentle kiss on her temple and smoothed his hand over her hair.

"When we leave here, we'll have to go back to separate bedrooms," she added reluctantly. "You know that, right?"

The lump in his throat was too huge to get past. So he just nodded and leaned his cheek against the top of her head.

"Ethan. I need to tell you…" Blythe paused and he wondered if she would finish. "I just wanted to say…"

Still she hesitated. It was so unlike Blythe that he reared his head back and lifted her chin with his finger so he could gaze into her eyes.

"Um. Please don't look at me like that. This is hard enough."

"Whatever it is can't be all that bad," he told her quietly. "I thought we'd at least become friends. You should be able to tell me anything."

He couldn't imagine what she had to say that would be so difficult. Blythe seemed perfect. She took most of life's glitches in her stride. Nothing ever appeared to faze her.

Well…maybe one or two of the things they'd done together over the last couple of nights might have rendered her speechless for that moment. But this was different. Something was bothering her and he didn't care to be shut out.

"Oh, never mind." She slid out of his arms and took a step back. "It's not that important. Can you arrange for our transportation back to L.A. while I go round up Ash?"

"Sure. But I think—"

"I appreciate it," she said, cutting him off. "This is one tough conversation I don't want to have. Ashley isn't going to be happy about leaving the ranch early. It'll be a tough trip for us both, getting there as fast as possible. And then there's her mother's condition. I don't know how she'll take that." With those words and one more sigh, Blythe smoothed her hands down over her jeans, gave him a quick smile and headed for the house.

Aroused, flustered and slightly annoyed at her, Ethan tried to imagine what kind of assistance would help her out the most. He couldn't do her job and talk to Ash. He couldn't even pack for her.

Going to L.A. was going to be tough on all of them. There must be something he could do to make it easier.

Blythe left Ash napping in the wide sleeper seat of the Delgado Ranch's corporate jet and moved down the aisle to talk to Ethan.

"Ethan Ryan," she whispered while slipping into the seat next to his. "You absolutely take my breath away. I can't believe you went to your father and arranged to have his jet fly us to L.A. this afternoon. How did you two get along when you saw him?"

"Okay." He shook his head. "For some reason I can't stay mad at him anymore. I'm not sure what happened to me. But all of a sudden, when I look at my father, the only thing I see is a lonely, sad man who's getting older every day. He's not the devil and the power-mad businessman wrapped into one nasty package that I used to know."

"Wow. That's really wonderful, Ethan. I'm a little surprised. But pleased. What do you think caused the change?"

"I have a feeling it's got something to do with you."

"Me? I haven't even had an opportunity to talk to you about giving your father another chance."

Ethan smiled wryly. "But you were going to, weren't you?" He didn't wait for an answer. "You don't have to say a word about how to do the right thing. Not when you live the example. Everything you do—with Ashley, with my sister and brother and his family, with Melissa and Max— all of it is honest and upright. You led me into becoming what you are. Ethical. Principled. A person worth knowing. That's what I'll strive to be from now on. Someone that others can count on to do the right thing. Someone like you."

Blythe was embarrassed. She didn't feel the least bit principled at the moment. In fact, she would love to take advantage of the lust between them to become a member of the mile-high club.

But that's not what she said. "I guess that's a compliment. Thank you. Though I'm sure the time was probably just right for you and your father to get past your old problems. After all, he is your father and I believe he cares for you very much."

"Well, I'm not sure I would go that far." Ethan chuckled and took her hand, linking his fingers with hers.

The spark was still there. It nearly made her cry.

At Maggie's this morning, before Max's phone call, she had been feeling so good. It wasn't just the sex. Or the way Ethan always made Ashley smile. Although both of those things couldn't be overlooked. The man was just basically a good guy with a strong, healthy—sexy—body and an excellent manner with all people, including kids.

No, it was more the way he treated them both in his everyday activities. As though they were the most outstanding, special and extraordinary females in the entire world. Blythe had never been treated that way. And she felt something inside her changing because of his unique attentions. She wasn't quite sure what was different yet, but she'd begun to feel…um…stronger.

Okay, so this morning she had chickened out of saying that she loved him. But that was only a minor backslide into the person she was before Ethan came into her life.

Blythe knew it was just a matter of time before she would tell him everything. She loved him. She wanted to shout it from the rooftops.

And yes, she was well aware the whole love deal was not his thing. The real reason she'd stopped herself this morning was that she hadn't wanted to see him get all embarrassed as he patiently explained once again about his vow not to fall in love after his family's curse. She'd known her one-sided declaration would make him feel guilty for her sake. He might have even pitied her just a little.

That had been the biggest sticking point as far as she was concerned. She couldn't bear to have the look in his eyes change from undisguised desire to cloaked pity.

But still she was determined to let him know the truth before he walked away from her for good. She *was* too honest and principled not to let him know he'd be walking away and taking her heart.

Blythe closed her eyes and let the warmth of his fingers seep through her body. She was facing a sad, difficult task when they reached L.A. and Ethan's strength would help see her through.

She wouldn't let herself dwell on their upcoming parting. That was for a future she didn't want to face just yet. A future she dreaded but would face with new inner strength. Thanks to Ethan.

Turning, she opened her eyes and faced him—for now. She gave him a small, sad smile and then asked him to tell her more about his magic and the protective charms.

It would be hard for her over the next week or two, seeing him every day but not being with him. However, she would handle it, as she did everything else.

Still, this was something she never thought she'd have to face again—being near the one she loved, only to know he could never truly belong to her.

Chapter 14

Ethan couldn't stand this part of his job. He was stuck waiting at Melissa's door while Ashley and Blythe spoke to the dying woman. He seldom had this much trouble doing his work. But watching their anguish and grief play out and not being able to comfort them was killing him.

He wanted to do something to make it better. But his magic didn't extend this far.

What he could do was just be here for them when they needed him. So he scanned the hallway, listened for signs of trouble from any quarter and waited.

"I'm sorry you're sick again, Mommy. Blythe says you might be dying. Is that true?" Ashley moved closer but didn't reach out to her emaciated mother, and Melissa didn't answer her question.

"We were having such a great time in Texas, Mommy. Lots of little kids live around Ethan's sister's house. Mostly smaller than me, but I was real good with the babies. And wait till I tell you about the horses. There was one named Zorro and one named Miss Molly, and I rode on Bobbie Jean. She was real gentle.

"Oh, Mommy, I had such a good—"

"Blythe." Melissa interrupted her daughter to speak to Blythe over her shoulder. "What is she talking about? You didn't let her near large animals, did you? The production company's insurance agent will have a fit if he learns Ashley was doing something dangerous. I thought you knew better than to allow her to be so foolish."

Blythe stepped closer, up beside Ashley. "We were careful, Melissa. She was never in any danger."

"Wait, Mommy. Wait until I tell you how much I love—"

"Shush, Ashley." Melissa's words to quiet the child were almost harsh. "Your mommy doesn't have much time. I want you to promise me you won't get into any trouble when I'm gone. I want your absolute vow that you will not embarrass me or the production company in any way. You have contracts to fulfill. They're like promises I've made on your behalf. You won't make Mommy look—"

"Where are you going, Mommy?"

Melissa shifted her head and looked up to Blythe. "You explain it to her later." Then Melissa turned one more time to pin her child with a withering look. "Give Mommy a kiss goodbye. Then I want that promise."

Ashley backed up a step. "No, Mommy. I don't want to act anymore. I want to live on the Delgado. I want to be a regular kid and ride horses and feed the chickens and take care of the babies. I love it there."

Melissa closed her eyes for a second, then blinked up at Blythe, the pain clear and present in her expression. "I want to speak to you. Right now. Send her away."

Blythe put her hands on Ash's shoulders and gently turned the child away from her mother's bedside. "Why don't you go downstairs and help Mrs. Hansen with dinner? I need to talk to your mother for a minute and then I'll be right down."

Ashley looked over her shoulder to where her mother lay, still and pale, in the bed. Then she straightened her lips in a narrow line, nodded to Blythe and plodded out the door. "Bye, Mommy."

Ethan knew he should follow the little star downstairs. She was, after all, his client. But he tilted his head when she passed him by to indicate she should go on without him. He wanted to stay here, where he could be within calling distance in case Blythe needed him.

The moment dragged out as Melissa lay quietly with her eyes still closed. When she finally opened them, she pinned Blythe with that same haughty stare.

"I trusted you," Melissa began in a hoarse whisper as she gripped Blythe's forearm with her bony fingers. "Backed you when you made a dreadful mistake. Was I wrong? Tell me I wasn't wrong."

"You weren't wrong, Melissa. I appreciate everything you've done. You can trust me. You know you can."

"I sincerely hope so. But remember, Max will be in charge of the money. If you make so much as one wrong move, both you and Ashley can be cut off without a cent. And he will see to it that you never work in Hollywood again. Good luck to you both then."

"It's not necessary to threaten me or your child." Blythe's voice was low and hard. "I will see to it that Ash lives up to her contracts. I gave you my word."

Ethan's fists balled at his sides. Damn Melissa. She was a sorry excuse for a mother if he'd ever seen one.

Still at Melissa's bedside, Blythe sighed heavily, trying to remember the other woman must be in terrible pain. Melissa Davis had not always been this way. Once she'd been a gorgeous, loving mother who wanted only what was best for her child. Regardless of what Ash had blurted out tonight, the little girl had always wanted to be an actress. Everyone said that, almost before she could walk, Ash could repeat lines from television shows. And when she did walk, she'd immediately started dancing and bowing for the applause. Blythe had seen the videos of her doing just that at age two.

Blythe waited as Melissa composed herself, wishing she could be downstairs with Ashley right now. The girl needed her. Melissa was beyond her help.

"Blythe." Melissa's voice was barely audible. "I'm sorry. I don't know why I act like such a… No, that's not true. It's jealousy. I've always wanted to be on-screen myself. Now there's no chance.

"And you…" Melissa reached her hand out in a gesture of helplessness and friendship, and Blythe took it in her own. "My daughter loves you more than she loves me. And I'm so jealous of you I can't stand it."

"That's simply not true, Melissa. Ash loves you very much. Why don't I get her back up here so the two of you can tell each other how you feel?"

Melissa shook her head. "Too tired now. Tomorrow." She closed her eyes. "We can say it all tomorrow."

But tomorrow never came for Melissa and Ashley. Later that night Melissa slipped into a coma. By 6:00 a.m. the doctor arrived to give her heavier medication and said he didn't think it would be too long. By noon, the once beautiful and loving mother left her pain-racked body behind on this earth and her soul found another place.

Max came and sat at her bedside for a long time after she died. Just sat, quiet and staring. Blythe checked on him a couple of times and worried that the funeral home should be called to pick up the body. In the meantime, she and Ethan and Mrs. Hansen tried to keep Ashley busy. There were other things they should be doing, and Blythe knew she needed to explain death and dying to Ash. But she didn't want to do it until after Melissa was out of the house.

Finally, while Ashley was taking a nap, Max came downstairs and said he had called the funeral home people and they would be there shortly.

"Melissa was very specific about her last wishes," Max told them. "She didn't want an open-casket service. She didn't want to be remembered looking this way. But she did want a huge showbiz-style funeral. All the bells and whistles. A big production number with people grieving."

Max chewed on his unlit cigar. "She died too young. People loved her. But not that many will remember the pretty mother of Ashley Nicole."

He sighed and screwed up his mouth. "I'll take care of everything. The cemetery has been expecting her for weeks. The funeral service will take place tomorrow."

On the one hand, Blythe thought the day was moving too fast. On the other hand, she would be glad, for Ashley's sake, to get this behind her. Blythe felt convinced that Ash needed to go back to work soon. The more the little girl stayed busy, the less time she would have to dwell on what could have been. The summer movie appearances were scheduled to start up again in Texas that night without her, and Blythe couldn't think of a better way for the child to keep her mind off her troubles. One or two more days at the most and Ash should rejoin the rest of the cast on the tour.

The wardrobe department at the studio found a suitable outfit for Ash to wear to the funeral when they visited there later that afternoon. Blythe still had not told the little girl about her mother's passing. She was having trouble thinking of the right thing to say. So she just kept them all busy.

Every once in a while, she would see Ethan studying her. He didn't seem too pleased. But maybe that was just her imagination.

That night, he stopped her in the hall after she'd put Ash to bed. "Just when are you going to tell the child her mother has died? The phone has been ringing off the hook. What if she hears about it from someone else?"

"I plan on telling her first thing in the morning. Before the funeral."

His eyes gentled as he brushed a stray hair from her face. "I know it's hard, sugar. I trust you to do the right thing. But can I help in any way? Should I be there for you?"

It was nice that he trusted her. But she wasn't so sure of herself. Her mind was whirling with possibilities. Right versus wrong. Commitment versus principle.

"No, but thank you, Ethan. This is something I have to handle myself. No help. No magic. Just straight-out guts."

He smiled and her heart warmed.

"Well, if you need me, or want to talk, just call."

He leaned down and kissed her lips. It was such an emotion-filled kiss, not hot at all, but so full of longing and tenderness that it made her chest ache.

What would she do when he wasn't there anymore? When the time came and she turned around to find no one there at all?

The next morning Blythe sat brushing Ashley's hair. She was taking Mrs. Hansen's place and getting Ash ready for the funeral so they could talk.

Blythe wasn't altogether positive Ashley should attend the funeral. Did seven-year-olds belong at cemeteries? But Melissa's last instructions were explicit. Torn, Blythe worked to convince herself that Ashley might feel bad forever if she wasn't allowed to say one last goodbye to her mother. It was as good an excuse as Blythe could think of for forcing a child to her mother's glitzy funeral.

Blythe just wished the whole thing didn't feel so much like a circus.

"Ash," she began. "You know how sick your mom's been?"

"Yes. My mommy hurts. She's dying."

"No, honey. Not anymore. Your mommy went to heaven. She won't ever hurt again. The reason we're getting all dressed up today is so we can attend her funeral. Do you know what a funeral is?"

Ashley stopped her usual fidgeting and looked into the mirror at Blythe's reflection. Blythe held her breath.

"My BFF, Stephanie—the one who starred in the movie with me, remember?—she said she had to go to a funeral last year. She didn't like it. Nobody smiled and some people cried—real tears, not fakes." Ashley shook her head. "I don't think I want to go. I want to talk to Mommy. She won't make me go."

"Ash…" Blythe reached for the little girl and pulled her to her chest. "You can't ask your mom. We won't be able to ask her anything ever again. She's gone. It's just the two of us now. Well…and Max and Ethan. We're all here for you."

Ash pulled back and studied Blythe's face but there were no tears. "My mommy died? Like my daddy did? She won't be coming back?"

"No, honey. But before she left she told me to tell you she loved you. Very much. She wanted you to know."

"But, Blythe, I didn't get to tell her—"

"Shush, Ash. It's okay. Your mommy knew. She knew you loved her. But right now we have to go to her funeral. She wanted us to be there."

"Will the newspeople be there, too?" Ash asked quietly. "They will, won't they? Mommy wants them there, too. I bet she does."

Blythe nearly bit her tongue to keep from crying—or from cursing Melissa's iron control from beyond the grave.

This was going to be horribly difficult for Ashley and it killed Blythe, having to force her to go. "I'm sorry, sweetie. Yes, I'm sure the newspeople will be there. But you don't have to talk to them if you don't want to."

Ash straightened up and flipped her hair off her shoulder, every bit the star actress. "That's all right, Blythe. I can do it. Mommy taught me how. I'm good at pretending."

Hours later as, hand in hand, Blythe was leading Ashley back to the limo from the grave site, she wished with all her heart that she had Ash's acting ability. This whole morning had been a terrible ordeal for Ash, and Blythe's heart cried out as she stuck with her through it all.

Ashley looked like a perfect child star today, dressed in a navy blue dress with a round white collar. Her perfect, long blond hair streamed down her back nearly to her waist. Her everyday photo makeup was all in place. Nothing had wilted in the hot sun. But Ashley still had not shed one tear. Blythe was concerned.

They followed the crowd along the curved path while the Southern California sun continued beating down on their bare heads. The air was laden with humidity for a change, so they waded through the soggy wind drafts as they passed by gravestones and garish mausoleums. A nice fog would have been more appropriate for a funeral, but apparently Melissa hadn't been able to order the weather to her specifications.

One more gauntlet and then they could go home. A news tent had been set up at the edge of the cemetery and the paparazzi were waiting to question the stars in attendance about their relationship to Melissa. Max had said he expected Ashley to say a few words. Melissa would have wanted it that way.

But Blythe didn't. The hordes of newsmen and photographers were shoving and shouting, trying to get the few grieving stars in attendance to make statements. Flashes exploded in blinding arrays. She looked over her shoulder to find Ethan, wondering if he would help them make an escape. He saw her looking and headed straight for them.

"You need something?"

"Yes. A way out."

Ashley looked up at them. "Mommy wants me to do this. I can. Maybe."

Ethan looked to Blythe. She just shrugged a shoulder and looked longingly toward the limo.

"Come on." Ethan gathered them both close, twisting them through the crowd in the direction of the limo. "None of us needs this aggravation. Not today."

But Blythe's indecision had cost them. A couple of the newsmen who'd been standing on the edges of the crowd caught sight of them and came running, shouting their inane questions and pointing cameras at a little girl who really shouldn't have been there in the first place.

All of a sudden Ashley pulled out of Blythe's grip and turned toward the cameras. She rubbed one of her tiny fists across her eyes and sobbed. Loudly.

Then she gazed up, right into the cameras and microphones, and said, "My mommy's dead. She's not ever coming back." Tears streamed down her cheeks and she folded her hands in front of her body, making her look like a cherub.

Blythe imagined it was an act, that Ashley was trying to deflect even worse questions. But it didn't work. The questions came anyway.

"How does it feel to be an orphan, Ashley Nicole?"

"Your fans want to know what it's like to lose a mother. Tell them all about it, Ashley."

Frantic, Blythe turned again to Ethan. "Please get her out of here."

Ethan nodded. He swung Ash up in his arms and shoved away from the ever-widening crowd, moving fast across the grass. Blythe tried to follow and had taken a few steps when she suddenly felt a tug on her arm. She was dragged around and came face-to-face with an old nightmare.

Howard Adams. The very last person she needed to see right now.

"How about an exclusive on this tragedy from the star's point of view?" he asked with one of his toothy grins.

"Not a chance, Howard. Let me go." She tried pulling her arm free, but he tightened his grip.

"I'll make it worth your while, Blythe. Besides, you owe me this."

Suddenly furious, Blythe gritted her teeth before answering, "I don't own you a damned thing. None of us does. Certainly not Ashley."

"Aw, come on. There's something seriously weird going on with her and you know it. How come she needs that big, bad bodyguard all of a sudden?"

"I *said* let go of me, Howard." Blythe was done with this jerk. He'd nearly ruined her life once. He was not going to waste another instant of her time ever again.

She tugged once more and when he didn't let go, she stomped down hard on his instep with her heel.

"Ow." Howard jumped and staggered back a step.

It was all the advantage she needed. She ran for the limo. But it was tough going on the grass in her pumps. The heels, though not as spiky as stilettos, kept sticking in the sod. She could hear Howard calling to her and closing in behind.

Then, in a whir of motion and movement, she felt herself being bodily picked up. The flash of energy and the surprise cost her a breath. When she took her next one, Blythe was sitting in the front seat of the limo as it slowly pulled away from the curb and the hordes of reporters surrounding it.

Ethan. He'd magically come to her rescue. Thank goodness.

It was two days after the funeral and Ethan couldn't believe they were back on the summer movie appearance trail. He and Blythe had barely had a moment alone to discuss future plans. Things seemed to be moving too fast, even for a guy like him, who usually liked to move in, get going, then back himself right out again.

But where was the time set aside for Ashley to adjust to her new circumstances? When would she grieve? He and Blythe had already had this argument once, right before they left L.A. He hadn't changed his mind a bit.

At the moment, Ash was signing autographs outside the Lubbock, Texas, mall while Ethan and Blythe stood together a few yards behind and watched out for her. Most of her little fans were expressing their sympathy but almost none of them could understand. At their tender ages they couldn't imagine doing without their own mommies.

Blythe seemed distracted. A few of the paparazzi had moved in behind the kids, circling like sharks. Ethan imagined Blythe wanted to keep Ash away from them as much as she possibly could.

He turned to Blythe. "What the hell are we doing here?"

"Ashley is working. It's her job. She has a contract. Remember?"

"Don't tell me the studio wouldn't have given her time off. Her mother just died, for God's sake."

"I made a promise, Ethan. I swore to Melissa on her deathbed. I live up to my promises."

Same old song. He still didn't buy it.

At that moment, a couple of aggressive mothers shoved their children right in front of Ethan and Blythe and blocked their view of Ash. Blythe took a couple of steps in the direction of the paparazzi. Ethan would've preferred to push past the crowd, but he knew his job didn't call for manhandling women and children.

"You know," he began, shifting to try to get Ash back in sight, "up to a few days ago I thought you were perfect. You always did the right thing. What happened? What you're doing now to that little girl isn't right and you know it. She needs time away from the bright lights. She's just a child, Blythe. Cut her some slack."

Blythe turned her face to him. Her eyes were shooting daggers, but behind the daggers was a sheen of sadness. He had to look away, back to his job.

"Don't tell me what—"

Ethan interrupted her by taking off at a run. Ash was not where she'd been just an instant ago. In fact, she was nowhere in sight.

Ashley was gone!

Chapter 15

At that moment twelve hundred miles away beside a tropical mountain lake in deepest Veracruz, Ethan's *Abuela* Lupe jerked to a halt in her herb garden. Something was very wrong. For the first time in longer than she could remember, her grandson Ethan had lost control and was in serious trouble. She could feel it. Knew it in her bones. Scented it in the air.

Ethan had always been the one she worried about the least. He was strong-willed and understood his heritage, living with the witchcraft but using it only for the right reasons. Ethan's world had always appeared so steady, yet now he seemed to be the one in trouble.

Clasping a few ruda plant leaves and some special magical twigs to her breast, Lupe made her way back to her modern brick house by the lake's shoreline. As a *curandera,* she could not interfere without a request. And she definitely refused to ask another favor of her mother, the *bruja.* The last favor the black witch had granted had ended with a man's death.

Lupe would not dare seek another dark favor, especially since she had already requested the ultimate favor her mother could ever grant. The only request that mattered anymore—having the curse lifted from her grandchildren's lives. And all the signs said that her wish would someday soon come to pass.

Still, she must do something for Ethan now. She would pray to Cruz de Caravaca for protection against all forms of evil. She would light the blue candle and use Ethan's photograph. She would pray: "Santa Cruz de Caravaca, I take refuge under your grandiose power so that your force distances from my grandson's life any wrong or illness that may trouble him."

And then, just to be sure, she would e-mail her grand-daughter Maggie for more information.

Blythe doubled over with fear. Where was Ashley?

Out of breath, she couldn't utter a word. But the look on her face must have told Ethan everything she'd wanted to say.

"She can't have gone far. She was there just an instant ago," he said as if he was in to mind reading. "We'll find her."

He began asking people who'd been in the vicinity if they'd seen where Ash had gone. It would be hard to miss Ashley Nicole. But no one had seen a thing. Finally, with Blythe trailing right behind him, Ethan went to the mall's front curb where the taxi stands were located.

Finding a security guard on duty, Ethan asked him if he'd seen a little blond girl.

"Lots of little girls around the mall today," the uniformed guard responded. "There's some big TV star who's signing autographs."

Ethan nodded that he knew. "This girl has long blond hair, almost to her waist, and is real pretty for a kid."

Blythe stepped around Ethan to face the guard. "Please, this is very important. Did you see a child that looked like she was in trouble?"

The guard studied her a moment. "Didn't I notice you over near that crowd of reporters earlier? The ones looking for interviews with the stars?"

Ethan stopped, turning to stare at her in the same way as the guard was doing.

"Um, yes. Why?" She'd only been looking through the crowd of paparazzi to see if that idiot Howard Adams had followed her all this way from L.A. And damned if she hadn't spotted him, too.

"Because now that you mention it," the guard answered. "I did see a little blond girl who seemed to be crying. She was leaving with one of those reporter guys. But it didn't look like she was in any trouble. In fact, the kid was holding the guy's hand."

Blythe's stomach twisted. "Was this reporter a good-looking man? About six feet with blond hair and a mouthful of white teeth?"

"Yeah. That's the guy."

"Oh God."

Ethan gripped her arm to keep her upright. "Did they leave in a cab?" he asked the guard.

"Naw. The guy had a van. Double-parked. He got away with a warning because of the crowds."

"Did you get the license?"

"Yeah. But it was a rental. I can give you that info, I guess."

Ethan took the information and then dragged Blythe away from the guard to a quiet corner. "Okay. Tell me."

She swallowed hard. Her hands were shaking and her legs trembled. How could something like this have happened? It was all her fault. Yet Ethan must be able to save Ashley. He would just have to.

"It's, uh…" She started over. "There's a reporter from L.A. named Howard Adams. About a year ago, he and I had a sort of fling."

"Fling?"

"Well, Howard pursued me. Sought me out and made a big play for me. Honestly, it turned my head. I was very foolish and let him into our lives when he promised to write a great magazine article about Ash. It was all very flattering—until I found out he was not really doing such a nice piece."

Blythe caught her breath and fought to turn a few of the worst months of her life into a few sentences. "His article was aimed at ruining Melissa. It made her look like a horrible and ruthless stage mother who traded favors to get her daughter into the spotlight.

"But that wasn't true about Melissa. She was smart and knew how to get ahead, but I don't believe for an instant she ever did the things he said. However…since I let him in, he claimed in the article to have the inside track."

Ethan just stood there and let her go on, though he was studying her with a look of skepticism she had never before seen on his face.

"When Melissa found out about the article, she and Max used their influence to get it buried, and to bury Howard, too. He was fired from his stringer job and Melissa swore he would never work for another decent magazine or paper again."

"And you saw him here today but didn't bother to mention it to me?" Ethan's voice was harsh, deadly.

"Yes."

"Let me get this straight." Ethan took her once again by the arm and pinned her with a dangerous look. "When you say you 'let him into' your lives, does that mean like with a key and the security code for the house?"

"Um…yes."

Ethan cursed and tightened his grip on her arm. "So Ashley's stalker could be this Adams dude, and he could've easily walked right into the mansion and used a house computer to send Ash that creepy message before I had all the codes and locks changed." It was not a question.

"I guess so. I forgot he still had a key."

Another barrage of expletives spewed from Ethan's mouth before he took a steadying breath. "Call the police. Wait here for them. Tell them everything. See if they'll issue an AMBER Alert. I'm going to find the bastard." He turned and started off.

"Ethan." What could she say? How would this ever be right again?

"What?"

"I'm sorry."

"Yeah," he said hastily. "Me, too. I should've known better."

A couple of hours later, Blythe had replied to question upon question by the many policemen who'd answered the child-missing call. But she didn't know if any of them were actually doing anything to find Ashley. And she hadn't heard a word from Ethan. Her guilt and frustration were mounting by the second. When one of the cops told her to meet them in their offices for further interviews, she nodded absently and headed for the limo.

As she walked to the lot to find Ash's limo driver, she decided to call Ethan to see what he'd found so far. When she opened her cell phone, she saw the blinking "voice mail waiting" sign. She must have been out of cell range inside the mall. Hopefully this call would be Ethan giving her good news.

But it wasn't Ethan's voice she heard when she retrieved her message. Instead it was a voice she'd hoped at one time to never hear again.

"Blythe," Howard said loud and clear through her phone. "I have Ashley with me. I just want to talk to you. This was the only way I could think of to get your attention."

Blythe heard an edge to Howard's voice that scared her senseless. This wasn't the same charming reporter she had known all too well. What was happening to him? And far worse, what was happening to Ashley?

"Listen," he continued. "I'm going to give you the address where I've got Ashley. I want you to come so we can talk. But if you bring the cops or tell them anything, I swear…" His voice trailed off and Blythe's heart raced. "Well, just don't tell them. I don't want to hurt anyone. But I will if I have to."

Blythe dug in her purse and tried to find a paper to copy down the address. The best she could come up with in a hurry was the back of a bank deposit slip from her checkbook. What had happened to the ever-prepared guardian in an emergency? she chastised herself.

She had to listen to the message twice to get it all straight. Then she stood, looking down at her cell phone as if it were a scorpion in her hand. What should she do? This kind of thing went far out of her experience. She needed professional help….

It didn't take her a second to punch in Ethan's direct-call button on her phone. But the call went directly to voice mail. *Damn.*

Deciding in that instant not to involve the police again, Blythe left Ethan a message. "Ethan, where are you? Howard just called. He says he has Ashley and not to let the police know where they are. He wants to talk to me. Uh, and here's the thing. If I do talk to him, and offer him an exclusive with Ash, maybe I can get him to release her. I can't really believe Howard will hurt Ashley. They had a decent relationship, before. I think this is all just a big stunt to get himself noticed again. I'm afraid the police will only complicate everything."

She repeated the address so Ethan could meet her there. After she hung up, Blythe said a little prayer that her decision was the right one, then turned and hopped into a cab.

Several miles away Ethan was saying his own prayers. He was probably making one of the stupidest mistakes of his life. And lately he'd made a couple of zingers.

This time, he was inside a news stringer's office—without the benefit of an invitation or a key. And he had been getting vibes that a silent alarm was going off. But he just needed another moment or two.

The car rental office had been forthcoming, after a little help from one of his hexes and some cash, with this temporary office as the current address for their rental van. Obviously, no one was living here. The reporters only used this place to file their stories and gather information.

But maybe he would find an address for Howard Adams if he could go through the rest of the desks and file cabinets. So far, he'd come up short. But in another minute…

The door he'd deliberately left unlocked banged open. "Lubbock police! Don't move!"

Ah, hell, Ethan thought as the holding cell doors slammed behind him. He didn't have time for this.

Being booked on a breaking-and-entering charge was the last thing he needed. The B and E charge was bogus, anyway. The police hadn't found any signs of forced entry, and they wouldn't, either. He'd made sure of that. Trespassing was the worst charge they eventually could make stick.

But the more urgent problem right now seemed to be that since it was Sunday, a judge would not be available to hear the charges until morning. There was no magic or hex or even curse that Ethan knew that would get him out any sooner.

Hell. He kicked at the wall and tried to think.

At least the cops here had been fairly respectful as they'd cuffed him, booked him and pitched him in the cell. Seemed everyone in every corner of Texas had heard the name Ryan, and they each knew that in Texas, it stood for the Delgado Ranch and all the power and history that implied.

With that single thought of the ranch, Ethan had another thought. One he wasn't sure was so smart. But under the circumstances, he was willing to try almost anything. The minute he was free and got his hands back on his cell phone, he would call Blythe. There had to be a way of locating Adams and Ashley that he hadn't thought of yet.

Rolling his shoulders, Ethan prepared to do something he had once sworn never to do. Then he called the guard and asked for a phone call.

He sure hoped one call was all it would take to locate Brody Ryan on a Sunday.

Chapter 16

"Blythe," Ashley whispered. The two of them huddled together in a corner of a crummy, out-of-the-way motel room. "What's the matter with Howard? He acts funny."

Blythe didn't want to answer because, truthfully, Howard looked and sounded insane. The minute Blythe had seen him and agreed to come inside his room to reach Ash, she'd become aware that Howard's mind had snapped. She would have snatched Ash up and made a run for it immediately, but Howard had produced a big handgun. Bigger than any she'd seen Ethan carry. And he'd said he would be forced to kill them both if they didn't sit quietly and give him a chance to think.

But Blythe wasn't so sure he was thinking, at least not clearly. The television blared from its spot on the dented dresser in the corner of the room while Howard paced, dug his fingers through his greasy hair and mumbled to himself.

Not that it was doing her any good, but she berated

herself for not waiting for Ethan. Or at least not having made another call to see if he'd received her message. She'd done so many things wrong over the past months. But her biggest regret was putting herself and Ash into this kind of danger without first making things right with him.

She hated that their last contact had been an argument.

He'd become the best part of her life. If she managed to live through this catastrophe, she would tell him so. And about how sorry she was for screwing up. How much better a person she was for having met him.

No matter that he was not her forever man—she'd always been aware that he could not possibly be hers to keep. Yet she wouldn't change a thing about their time together.

Except maybe for the last few hours.

Ashley snuggled closer and Blythe realized she had another person who needed to hear all those things, as well. One who also needed for her to stay strong.

"Ash, why did you leave with Howard?" Blythe asked softly. She still couldn't understand how they'd gotten into this spot. "Didn't you remember what I told you about only taking orders from either me or Ethan?"

"Oh, but Howard didn't make me go. I asked him to take me."

"Take you where? The limo was waiting to take you wherever you wanted to go." What was Ash saying?

"I knew you wouldn't let them take me to the Delgado," she mumbled into Blythe's shoulder. "Howard said yes. But then he said we had to stop here first. I don't like it here. I want out."

The Delgado. Suddenly everything was clear to Blythe—and she didn't like what she was seeing. Ethan had been right to worry about pushing Ash too hard after her mother's death.

Blythe slid a protective arm around Ash's shoulders and

hugged her close. "You were going to the ranch without me? Oh, Ash. Why couldn't you have talked to me about it first?"

Ashley reached up and patted her face. "Don't be upset, Blythe. I was going to call and get you to come, too. I wouldn't want to be there alone.

"But when I heard you and Ethan arguing about going there, I thought it was because you loved each other. I thought if I went there first, you both would have to come, too. And make up."

Now the tears welled in earnest in Blythe's eyes. Man, did she ever owe Ethan a big apology! Blythe was going to tell him the first chance she got. And she *would* get that chance. She swore she would. There would be some way for her and Ash to escape this place.

"Ashley, I love you. Do you know that?" She placed a kiss on top of the silky blond head.

"Sure, Blythe. I know. I love you, too. Now can we go? Make Howard let us out."

Ashley didn't mention the gun, thank God. Maybe she thought it was a joke or a prop.

"Give me a few minutes, honey. I have to talk to Howard first. But I want you to quietly go lock yourself into the bathroom while we talk. Can you do that for me?"

"Okay. Are you a-scared of Howard? Should I try to crawl out the window in there—like in the movies?"

"Under no circumstances, Ashley Nicole Davis. We're on the second floor here. I just want you to stay quiet and be safe."

Blythe cleared her throat and called to Howard. He stopped pacing, but when he looked her way, his eyes were wild and too bright. His hair was spiked up in unnatural peaks from running his hands through it. His clothes were a little grungy and when he took a step closer, she knew he hadn't bathed in a long while.

"Ashley needs to use the bathroom. Okay?"

He shrugged but put his hand on the gun in his waistband.

"Go," she whispered to Ash. "Lock the door and lie down in the bathtub."

Ashley obeyed without a word. Then Blythe turned to face an evermore frightening Howard. She had to engage him in talk. Had to distract him so she could get to her purse and her cell phone.

"Howard, why are you doing this? What did Ashley and I do that would make you so mad at us?"

He stepped over and put his filthy fingers against her cheek. The smell brought more stinging tears to her eyes.

"You two are just collateral damage. I don't have anything against you. Not really."

She jerked her cheek away from his hand and he snarled in response.

"Maybe," he began with a leer in her direction. "I would like to finish what you and I started once. And maybe we'll get the chance before I have to kill you. But it's Max and Melissa who need to pay. I already tried the revenge route, but that failed. This time everyone dies."

Oh God. He was truly crazy.

"Howard, Melissa is dead. You know that. And you aren't really going to kill me or Ashley. Are you? I think I once meant—"

"You never meant anything. How could you? Just look at you. It was all an act. Every bit of it. I should get some kind of award. I came after you to hurt them, and it almost worked. If you hadn't turned on me at the last second, I would've ruined them both and made them pay. Why should I care about you now? You're just another prop to use to get to Max."

"What did Max ever do to you?" Blythe was really frightened now. Her knees were trembling and she had to hide her hands under her armpits so he wouldn't see how badly they shook.

"Oh, nothing much," he said with a casual shrug. "Only ripped out my soul with his promises and his dreams. I wanted to give him back that same kind of pain. I want him to know what it is to suffer. The man is the devil and I intend to stop him forever."

Blythe was not only scared, but she was fast becoming panicked. Howard was too crazy to reason with. She had to find a way to get Ashley out.

Keep him talking. "What did Max do to you? I don't understand. Did he promise you something?"

"Not me," Howard tossed back at her. "The woman I loved. The only woman..."

"Come on, witch," he snapped, and grabbed at her arm. "Let's call your friend Max. See if he remembers. See how he likes hearing the cries of someone he loves while they lie dying and he can't do anything to help them. Let's just see how he feels then."

She gasped for air, trying to remain calm enough to keep him talking. "Howard, please. First explain it to me. Tell me what happened. Maybe I can think of a way to help."

He went to the table, picked up her purse and dumped the contents. "Here. Use your phone and call him. Tell him he'd better listen. This is going to be fun."

Outside the motel, Ethan sat behind a growing police barricade in the backseat of a cruiser belonging to the Texas Rangers. He was listening to his sister on the other end of his cell phone.

"I have *Abuela* Lupe now on both the phone and instant message," Maggie told him. "*Abuela* knew something was very wrong and she swears she can help."

Ethan figured he would be eternally grateful to his father

for bailing him out so quickly and for putting him in touch with the Texas Rangers. And he would also be forever grateful to Blythe for leaving him that message with the motel's address. Now he would be more than just grateful if *Abuela* Lupe's witchcraft could help him save the two people who had come to mean everything to him.

He hadn't taken a breath in an hour and his heart had stopped cold the moment he'd heard Blythe's message on his voice mail. The stalker had possession of both pieces to his world. Ethan wanted them back.

"The police are about to contact the stalker, Maggie. The man's cut the phone line to his motel room, but they think they can reach him by Blythe's cell."

"*Abuela* Lupe wants to know if you gave Ashley a protection charm." Maggie's voice was clear across the miles.

"Tell her yes."

"Then she says to go around behind and pull her free. The child is waiting."

Ethan didn't question his grandmother's information or bother to ask where or how. Keeping the phone line to his sister open, he slipped away from the cruiser and inched around behind the motel. Another group of cops were set up there, but he spotted a Texas Ranger he knew. Ethan had on a Ranger's jacket, given to him by one of the SWAT team members who knew he was ex-Secret Service. No one seemed to be paying attention to him. They were all focused on the motel.

When he closed in on the guy he'd met earlier, Ethan gave a nod toward the second story of the motel. "One of those upstairs windows belong to the target room?"

"Third from the left. Small. Probably a bathroom window."

"Can we get up there?"

"If we were sure the perp wouldn't blow our heads off first, yeah." The cop motioned to a stack of construction materials next door. On the side was an extension ladder.

"How about I give it a try?"

The cop gave him a sharp once-over. "You won't make it through the opening even if you live to get there."

"Just hold the ladder for me, pal." Under his breath, Ethan said a quick hex that would keep these Rangers helping and not hindering him.

Then Ethan put the phone back to his mouth. "Mags, ask *Abuela* to start a spell that I can't manage on my own. I need for Ashley and Blythe to know I'm on the way."

There was agreement from the other side of the connection. Ethan set to work.

Once he had gently put the ladder in place against the wall, he climbed two rungs and heard a noise. Looking toward the sound, he saw the window inching upward. It was creaking more loudly than he would've wished. But within a few seconds, he spotted Ash's blond hair.

He scrambled up the rungs to the second story. "Ash. It's me. Can you get out the window?"

"Ethan? Blythe told me not to."

"It's okay, honey. I'll help you out."

"What about Blythe? She's in *there* with him and I locked the door."

"Unlock the door, Ash. Real quietly. But don't open it. Then come back and hurry out the window to me. I'll make sure Blythe makes it out."

Ashley did as he asked and he helped her climb from the window and then carried her to the ground. He handed her to the waiting Ranger. "Ashley, stay with this man. I'll get Blythe and meet you in few minutes."

"Are you sure, Ethan? I want Blythe." As good as she'd been, Ash's eyes began tearing up and her nose turned red. These looked like very real tears to Ethan.

"I know, baby. I promise. I've never broken a promise, have I?"

Ashley shook her head and backed up a step. Ethan made sure she was safe with the Ranger, then he returned to his phone.

"Maggie, what can *Abuela* do to help now? Can she make Blythe move into the bathroom alone?" Ethan wasn't absolutely positive Blythe could make it through the bathroom window, but if it was possible to hex it or curse it or physically battle it out of the way, he meant to have her free of that room.

"Hey, buddy." One of the police team members had a radio to his ear and was motioning to him. "The SWAT captain in front can't reach the perp by phone. They're going to try the blow horn now, and they want to know if you're positive there's only one hostage left in that room."

Hostage. Blythe was a hostage. Images of their time together zipped through his mind like a slide show on fast forward. Picturing reams of her curls lying softly against his pillow, and thinking of her easy, sexy smiles and expectant, loving expressions cost him a moment—and some pangs of terror.

"I'm positive. And I think I can get her to move into the bathroom out of the line of fire if your guys can keep Adams busy with a diversion in the other direction. Let me try?"

The cop relayed the message and nodded the affirmative.

Ethan went back to his phone for one more shot at getting help. "Mags, what does *Abuela* Lupe say now?"

"She says your woman is bright and brave and it's no wonder you love her. The moment she can, Blythe will appear where you wish her to be."

"I don't…" His automatic response to the *L* word would have to wait. He needed to save Blythe before everything else.

Turning, he started back up the ladder. But then, from the far side of the building, shots rang out. *Blythe.*

He climbed to the window in an instant, just in time to see curls of smoke snaking free of the window sash. Taking a whiff, Ethan knew the cops had fired either tear gas or smoke bombs or both into the room as a diversion. His eyes teared up, but that wouldn't stop him from going inside. Where was Blythe?

His upper body was almost totally inside the tiny bathroom by the time Blythe appeared like an ethereal vision through the smoke screen mists. "Ethan?" she said over her raspy coughs. "I heard you calling my name. Help me."

Stretching out his hands, he dragged her to the window and backed himself out, bringing her almost all the way with him. "You can make it, too, darlin'. Try."

Ethan hadn't been calling her name, at least not consciously. No matter. The most important thing was to set her free. He began saying a series of hexes and prayers he thought might help them in this situation and coaxed Blythe to climb out the window.

He should've had more faith in his own magic, or maybe more faith in his grandmother and Blythe, because within moments he somehow had Blythe in his arms and back on the ground. Running with her half slung over his shoulder, he moved them away from the motel just as flames broke free from the upstairs windows. The immediate sounds of fire trucks in the distance told him the Texas Rangers had known there would be a fire—probably because they'd used dangerous smoke bombs. Blythe had gotten out just in time.

When he heard her gulping in clean, fresh air…when he felt her breath, warm and alive against his neck…when he held her to his chest and sensed the beating of her heart in time with his own—that's when Ethan Ryan took his first real breath since the whole ordeal had started.

She was safe. His heart would not stop today.

Three days later, on a beautiful morning with a clear sapphire-blue Texas sky, his heart had almost settled back into its normal pace. The moment he'd been able to, Ethan had bundled up Ashley and Blythe and brought them to the Delgado to stay with Maggie. Although neither of them had been physically injured, both of them were in shock and still had nightmares. For them, every shadow contained ghosts of terror and echoes of panic.

His sister's healing spirit was beginning to work wonders on them. But now Ethan had some news to give Blythe, and he sure hoped she was well enough to hear it. He had waited until Maggie took baby Emma and Ashley next door to play with her friend Lara's day-care children. The house was empty except for the two of them.

He found Blythe sitting at Maggie's kitchen table drinking coffee and poured himself a mug to join her. "I've just gotten word from the Texas Rangers. Howard Adams died of burns and smoke inhalation in the hospital last night. They thought you and Ashley should know he won't ever harm you again."

Blythe shot him a glance over the rim of her coffee mug and then set it down to talk to him. "I'll find a way to tell Ash. I'm sorry they couldn't save Howard, but I'm grateful she won't have to make statements or testify against him. I'd like for her healing to go on uninterrupted. I've been making some headway in having her understand that none of this was her fault."

Ethan put a hand over hers. "You understand that, too, right?"

She nodded but her eyes still carried that slightly bruised look they'd had since he'd freed her and Ash.

"So, can you tell me what you've learned about Adams's motive?" he asked, hoping talking about it would help her. "I never got the whole story."

"I had a long talk with Max on the phone last night," Blythe began while she stared down into her coffee. "He wanted permission to come visit Ash. He's been beside himself with worry. I told him she was okay, to stay home and that we'd see him soon. He filled in the details of Howard's story for me."

"Can you talk about it?"

She gave him another quick glance and nodded. "Turns out I wasn't even a bit player in Howard's story. He was always using me, only I didn't know the real reasons."

With a sigh she went on. "Up until a couple of years ago, Howard was engaged to marry a woman he'd been in love with since they were children. He followed her out to Hollywood because she wanted to be in the movies. But she wanted that more than she wanted to marry Howard. She was only leading him on and letting him pay her way.

"I guess this woman also caught Max's eye, and he thought she had some talent," Blythe continued. "In hindsight from Max's point of view, he says he didn't feel he made her any promises. However, apparently she was absolutely convinced Max would make her a star."

Blythe stopped to take a sip of coffee and sadly shook her head. "Old and corny but still a sad story.

"Around that same time Max got ready to semiretire and decided he would devote his time to Ashley…and to convincing Melissa to begin her own career in the movies."

"Melissa? Really?"

"Yes. Max says the camera loved her face and she could have been great at acting. Melissa was a natural. That's how she taught Ash. So anyway, Max dropped this other woman flat. He wasn't interested. She was devastated."

"How devastated?" Ethan had a feeling he knew.

"The worst. When she couldn't interest any other big-name managers into taking her on, she committed suicide. Didn't even bother to leave Howard a goodbye message."

Ethan actually felt a pang of sympathy for Adams before he remembered that the idiot had threatened to hurt the ones he cared about. "So this dude Adams turns around and decides to take revenge on Melissa and Max for his girl-friend's death? Sounds to me like both Adams *and* his woman had more than a little trouble recognizing reality."

Blythe smiled. It was the first real smile he'd seen on her face in days and it warmed him all the way down to his boots.

She reached over, took his hand in hers and squeezed. "I never got a chance to thank you for saving Ash and me."

"Just doing my job, ma'am." He tried a grin, but he wasn't sure it came out right.

Blythe's smile turned into something he could've sworn looked a lot like longing. "I'm in love with you."

The words echoed in his head. The punch to his gut left him sputtering.

"Oh." She laughed uneasily. "Don't waste your breath with saying how you can't love me back because you're cursed, or try using the old 'I'm not cut out for marriage' line."

She was chuckling at him now and it pissed him off.

"I do not expect you to love me back," she said. "And I certainly have no intention of getting married. I have a re-sponsibility to Ashley and that leaves no room for marriage."

Well now, that speech called for some response, but un-fortunately his brain was still hung up on the *L* word.

"Look, sugar," he managed. "You've been under a lot of pressure. There's this condition called an adrenaline high. That's probably—"

"I know what I feel," she said with a snap of temper. "I've been trying to find a way to tell you since before we left the Delgado the last time. But I didn't mean to trap you and I'm certainly not hinting for a ring. I'm never doing the marriage thing again."

He'd forgotten she had been married once before. "You've been there and didn't like it?" The relief he felt reverberated in his voice.

Her lips twitched into a wry grin. "My ex was just another user. Only married me so my father would help him get tenure at the university. Once he felt settled enough, the jerk dropped me and found someone pretty. Typical.

"No, I don't need to pin my dreams on some guy anymore, thank you. But that doesn't also mean I don't love you." She blinked a couple of times and Ethan's gut started wrenching. "I have never loved anyone like I love you. I just felt you deserved to know."

Without realizing what he was doing, Ethan pulled her against him and hugged her hard. But he was too shaken to kiss her. Too stunned to say a word. The silence dragged on too long.

Maybe by tomorrow he would think of the right thing to say to make her understand what he couldn't come to grips with himself just yet. Yeah, that had to be a plan. Today he would think it over. Tomorrow they would talk.

So he found a polite way to bid Blythe goodbye for the moment, and then he went off to the Delgado alone to consider.

But the next day when the sun was high in the sky and Ethan went back to Maggie's after thinking throughout the night, he found that all his worry and considering—all his carefully chosen words—were worth exactly nothing.

Blythe and Ashley were long gone. Back to L.A. without so much as a goodbye. And he almost knew how Howard Adams must've felt.

Devastated.

Chapter 17

Maggie Ryan drove her rental car past the security gate and up to the front door of Ashley's mansion in L.A. She'd had enough. Six weeks since Blythe and Ash had left the Delgado, and it'd been six weeks of pure agony. Maggie intended to end it right here.

Her middle brother had become impossible to live with. Storming around with a scowl on his face. Moping around mumbling to himself, "It's all for the best. We're all better off."

Well, hell, no, they were not *all* better off. No one seemed better off with things the way they stood.

Maggie parked and knocked on the door. She had called ahead when her plane landed and made an appointment to see Blythe and Ashley. Now she just hoped she could make Blythe really *see* how things stood, and then make them different.

Blythe came to the door and immediately Maggie knew

she'd been right to come to L.A. Here, clearly, was the other half of the broken hearts club.

"Come in and sit down," Blythe told her. "Would you like some iced tea?"

Maggie sat and accepted an icy glass. Inside she was smirking. There was nowhere else on earth where people made sweet iced tea the way they did on the Delgado Ranch. She'd taught Blythe how to make it herself, and was pleased and surprised to see the other woman hadn't forgotten.

"How is Emma?" Blythe asked.

"The baby's fine. I'm still looking for any extended relatives so I can be sure it's okay to adopt her. But I haven't had much luck. It's becoming frustrating."

Blythe reached over and patted her hand in sympathy. "It'll work out. I know how much you love her."

Speaking of children we love... "Where's Ash? I miss her so much."

"She had a costume fitting this afternoon. Mrs. Hansen is with her. I thought you and I could talk before she gets back. She'll be pleased to see you."

"I'm glad to know you feel it's safe enough now to let her out of your sight. I did notice you still had a security guard at the gate."

Blythe smiled, but her expression was wane and slightly wary. "The guards are just to keep the paparazzi off the grounds. For the most part the reporters have given up trying to get Ash to talk to them, but she still can't stand to be around them. They remind her too much of Howard.

"Maggie, why are you really here? Is something wrong?"

"Blythe, are you happy?" Answering a question with another question might be slightly rude, but her new friend looked so miserable.

"Um...not really." She sighed and shrugged. "But we're getting along. I imagine it will just take more time."

"Are you still in love with my brother?"

Blythe blanched at the question, but she kept eye contact. "Yes, for all the good it does me."

"Have you ever thought of coming back to give him another chance? Maybe after being apart for all this time, he might've changed. I know I said he couldn't get past the idea of being single, but time has a way of bringing the important things into focus."

"Is he all right? He's not sick, is he?"

"Just sick in the heart," his sister muttered to herself. Louder, she said, "No, he's fine. He's been losing a little weight, but I see you have, too."

Maggie could also see that Blythe was eager for any word of the man she loved. "Ethan's been keeping busy. He's still helping Josh and me with the security business and he's been learning the oil business from our dad in his spare time. But…"

"You think he might run the Delgado oil business eventually? It's wonderful that he and your father are getting along so well."

"Hmm. They have an armed truce kind of relationship. They're still too much alike. But Dad thinks Ethan should be the one to run the business when he retires, and I tend to agree.

"But," Maggie added quickly, "I'm being serious. Would you consider coming back to Zavala Springs? You and Ash can live with me while you and Ethan discover whether things are still the same. There's tons of room at my house. And if you think you need something more than Ashley to keep you busy, the town is in dire need of teachers. We could use your help."

A ghost of a smile played across Blythe's lips, but it never reached her eyes. "I might be willing to take the chance on having your brother turn me down yet again, if it was only me I had to think about. But there's Ash…."

"Is Ashley happy here?"

Blythe shook her head. "Not really. I know she would give anything to be back on the Delgado. She only pretends to be happy here because she thinks that's what I want."

"Well then, do it for Ash." For all of us, Maggie thought miserably. "Move to Zavala Springs and give my idiot brother one more chance to not screw up his life entirely. Give Ash a chance to have a real childhood."

Blythe's expression became wistful, but bleak. "I admit, it's tempting. Hollywood has lost whatever appeal it ever had for me and Texas seems perfect. But we can't move now. Ash still has to finish out her contract with the studio. She has the rest of this season to shoot and then one more year. Maybe after that…"

"You can't tell the production company you want out of her contract? What does Max say about this? Does he know Ash isn't happy anymore?"

"I think Max does know—deep down. But he and I promised Melissa. And if Ash simply reneged on her contract, Max wouldn't be able to hold his head up in this town. Then none of us would be happy. Ash wouldn't want to hurt him."

Frustrating, Maggie thought. But she was also having glimmers of an idea.

"So are you saying you would move to Zavala Springs now if you could? And that you will definitely plan on coming when Ash's contract is finished?"

"Hey, you're pretty pushy, you know that?" Blythe said with a chuckle. "Yes, I would like to come now, but I can't. Though I will give it a lot of thought for later."

"Well, I have an idea that might speed things up a bit. Would you consider coming sooner than two years if I can put together a plan?"

"Don't tell me you're planning on trying a charm or

hex?" Blythe smiled but she looked worried. "Please say you don't intend to call in your grandmother."

"No. But I know someone who can help."

Ethan shoved his shaving kit into his duffel and slung it over his shoulder. He'd made up his mind. Eight weeks since he'd last seen Blythe, and he wasn't sleeping any better now than he'd been when she first left.

Maggie had snuck off to check on Ash and Blythe a couple of weeks ago. But this was his time. He was on his way to California.

He was tired of eating alone. He was sick and tired of drawing house plans for his section of the Delgado only to discover himself penciling in Blythe's and Ashley's names on every room. He had spent his very last minute ever tossing around in the guesthouse's huge bed, reaching out for Blythe only to grab hold of nothing but air.

There was every chance that Blythe had changed her mind and didn't love him anymore. He wouldn't blame her. He had been a first-class fool to let her words of love go unanswered when he'd known in every fiber of his being that he returned the emotion.

He'd thought about calling her, only every minute of every day for eight full weeks. But somehow, he couldn't bring himself to say what he must say over the phone.

There was no choice for him at this point. He didn't want to go on this way anymore.

He was fully prepared to set up residence in California if she thought she needed more time. He would give her anything, if there was the slightest chance of keeping her love. The only thing he wasn't ready for was if she sent him away. That might kill him.

Dialing his cell, he called his father. "Dad," he began

when the old man answered. "Can I use the corporate jet this morning?"

"It won't be back until late today," his father answered. "I sent the crew on an errand."

"Oh? Well, later, then."

Ethan talked a few more minutes to his father and got his permission for a ride to L.A., but something seemed off about his dad today. Ethan couldn't quite put his finger on it.

Setting down his duffel, Ethan shrugged off the odd feeling and prepared to spend another miserable twenty-four hours without a heart.

At seven o'clock that same night, Ethan showed up at the airstrip with his duffel again in hand. He'd called earlier and had gotten two new pilots lined up to fly him westward after the jet was refueled and checked out.

He couldn't stand to cool his heels back at the guesthouse for one more minute, so he'd come out to wait for the plane. He wouldn't mind waiting in the tiny shack next to the hangar at the airstrip. Hanging out for a couple of hours here was infinitely better than staying another second in the place where he and Blythe had spent so many happy hours together.

Something out of place caught his eye as he walked away from the ranch's Jeep. He figured he was seeing things. He hadn't had enough sleep lately and his eyes were playing tricks. There seemed to be more action than usual in the hangar tonight. What he'd seen could've been anything. It made him wonder what kind of errand his father had sent the crew on earlier.

Once more, a glimpse of something silvery blond flashed under the bare bulbs of the bright overhead lights in the hangar. This time, he knew he wasn't seeing things.

Dropping his duffel, Ethan took off at a trot. That much blond hair could not possibly belong to anyone but Ashley.

"Ash," he called out as he rounded the plane and spotted her standing there.

When she saw him, Ashley rushed in his direction. "Ethan! Oh, Ethan, we're finally here!" She flew into his outstretched arms.

He smothered her with kisses and hugged her fiercely. "Yes, baby, you're here. But I don't understand."

Looking over her head, he said, "Where's Blythe?"

"She's coming." Ash turned her head back toward the plane. "There. See?"

Yes, he did see. There. His heart.

The woman he'd been dreaming about and stewing over came down the ramp and headed in their direction. He held his breath as she walked toward him and Ash.

God, she looked good. Her hair was a little shorter, but it still floated around her head like a cloud. She was wearing dress jeans and a short denim jacket, and she walked with a high head and a determined step. Slim and sophisticated looking, she seemed changed. Had her feelings changed, too?

Still, she'd come all this way for some reason. He swiped at his blurry eyes with his shirtsleeve so he could see her better. When he looked again, she was still there and smiling.

"Hi," she said hesitantly. Then she turned to Ash. "Honey, I need to talk to Ethan a moment. Go into that office where the pilot just went and wait for us. Okay?"

"But, Blythe, I want to talk to Ethan, too…." Ashley must've seen something in Blythe's expression because she quickly gave in. "Oh, okay."

When the child was out of earshot, both he and Blythe began at the same time.

"Your father bought out Ash's contract," she began. "He must really have some kind of heavy-duty influence."

"I'm sorry about the way things ended between us," Ethan said at the same time. "Wait. What did you just say?"

"Your father contacted Max and the two of them came up with a way for everyone to win. The studio got big bucks for Ash's contract. Max found a new child actress to take her place. And Ashley is free to stay on the Delgado for as long as you…" Blythe finally wound down and stared at him. "What were you starting to say?"

They could discuss all the details of what and how later. And he could swear at his father for not hinting at what was going on—much later. This was the time for the big picture, which he'd been preparing to confess for weeks now. He just wished his knees were steadier.

Maybe he would do better if he could touch her and be sure she was real. Reaching out, he drew her closer and took both her hands in his own.

"I love you," he said, and wished his voice was stronger. So he said it again. "Blythe Cooper, I love you. I never thought I would say those words to anyone whose name isn't Ryan or Delgado, but it's the damned truth.

"I'm only sorry I didn't say it before. When it mattered most. My excuse is just that I'm a sorry-ass bastard. And I wouldn't blame you for never speaking to me again."

She just kept staring at him and his heart thumped in his chest. God, she couldn't have already changed her mind about loving him, could she? He didn't think he could stand hearing her try to brush him off.

"Ethan, I—"

He cut her off with a searing kiss. It started as a way to keep her from saying something he didn't want to hear, but as their lips touched, he lost control.

Every thought, every emotion went into his kiss. *Please love me back,* he begged with his whole body. *Please don't leave me again.*

At last he got his spine back and gently broke the kiss. But he kept his gaze locked on her gorgeous face for any sign.

She opened her eyes and blinked up at him. "I came here to give us another chance. I thought, given enough time, maybe…But now…"

His heart stopped beating again. *Please.*

"I love you, too," she added hurriedly. "That hasn't changed one bit with time. And as far as I can tell it isn't going to vary for this entire lifetime. So if you're sure—"

"I love you," he broke in. "I love you. I swear, I'll love you for this lifetime and many more. No curse has the power to change that or break us apart. Just stay with me. You and Ashley are my heart. The three of us need to make a life together."

When she just nodded, he kissed her again and vowed to tell her how beautiful she was and how much he loved her every single day for the rest of their lives. He had finally found a reason to care about the family's curse.

But now, he'd discovered that with the right woman, it really didn't matter.

Epilogue

With a heavy heart and hands full with simple, sweet treats, *Abuela* Lupe slowly climbed her mother's mountainside. In her late nineties, her mother, the black witch, had finally gone totally blind. Life was slowly ebbing away from the Veracruz *bruja*.

Yet Lupe felt certain there would be enough time left to save her mother's soul. Maria Elena Ixtepan had already begun refusing to sell curses and hexes for her old clients. That was a start. But a true change of heart would mean finding a forgiving spirit.

A true change of spirit would come when the old black witch recanted her curse on the Ryan children. Lupe wanted that more than anything. She wanted her children free of their curse, and she wanted her mother to feel the blessings of forgiveness before she died.

There was a better chance today than yesterday. Lupe was coming to tell her mother that Brody Ryan had performed a second good deed. He had gone to great difficulty in order to bring a child her heart's desire, and at the same time to give a young woman and his son a second chance at finding their own happiness.

This was Brody's second good deed. And Lupe's mother had promised that with three sincere deeds, she would reverse the curse.

Lupe could only hope that his third good deed would come soon. The magical sands of time were slowly fading, and Lupe wanted nothing more after her mother was gone than a new beginning for everyone.

* * * * *

Maggie Ryan yearns to adopt baby Emma.
But the baby's uncle is an unexpected—
and thoroughly unsettling—complication.
Don't miss the final story of The Safekeepers,
IN SAFE HANDS,
available in April 2009.
Only from Linda Conrad and
Silhouette Romantic Suspense!